play *acoustic guitar* *with...*
20 great hits

GW00503988

Wise Publications
London/New York/Sydney/Paris/Copenhagen/Berlin/Madrid/Tokyo

Published by
Wise Publications
14-15 Berners Street,
London W1T 3LJ, UK.

Exclusive Distributors:
Music Sales Limited
Distribution Centre, Newmarket Road,
Bury St Edmunds, Suffolk IP33 3YB, UK

Music Sales Pty Limited
120 Rothschild Avenue,
Rosebery, NSW 2018,
Australia.

Order No. AM976734
ISBN 0-7119-9859-0
This book © Copyright 2003 Wise Publications,
a division of Music Sales Limited.

Music arranged by Arthur Dick.
Music processed by Andrew Shiels.
Cover design by Chloë Alexander.
Printed in the EU.

CDs recorded, mixed and mastered by Jonas Persson.
All guitars by Arthur Dick.
Bass by Paul Townesend.
Keyboards by Paul Honey.
Drums by Brett Morgan.

Your Guarantee of Quality
As publishers, we strive to produce every book to the highest commercial
standards. The music has been freshly engraved and the book has been
carefully designed to minimise awkward page turns and to make playing from
it a real pleasure.
Particular care has been given to specifying acid-free, neutral-sized paper
made from pulps which have not been elemental chlorine bleached. This pulp
is from farmed sustainable forests and was produced with special regard for
the environment.
Throughout, the printing and binding have been planned to ensure a sturdy,
attractive publication which should give years of enjoyment. If your copy fails
to meet our high standards, please inform us and we will gladly replace it.

www.musicsales.com

Guitar Tablature Explained

Guitar music can be notated three different ways: on a musical stave, in tablature, and in rhythm slashes.

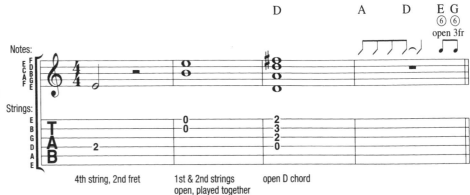

RHYTHM SLASHES are written above the stave. Strum chords in the rhythm indicated. Round noteheads indicate single notes.

THE MUSICAL STAVE shows pitches and rhythms and is divided by lines into bars. Pitches are named after the first seven letters of the alphabet.

TABLATURE graphically represents the guitar fingerboard. Each horizontal line represents a string, and each number represents a fret.

4th string, 2nd fret   1st & 2nd strings open, played together   open D chord

Definitions For Special Guitar Notation

SEMI-TONE BEND: Strike the note and bend up a semi-tone (1/2 step).

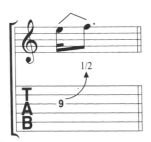

WHOLE-TONE BEND: Strike the note and bend up a whole-tone (whole step).

GRACE NOTE BEND: Strike the note and bend as indicated. Play the first note as quickly as possible.

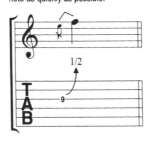

QUARTER-TONE BEND: Strike the note and bend up a 1/4 step.

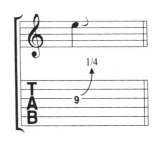

BEND & RELEASE: Strike the note and bend up as indicated, then release back to the original note.

COMPOUND BEND & RELEASE: Strike the note and bend up and down in the rhythm indicated.

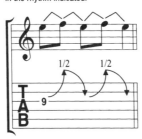

PRE-BEND: Bend the note as indicated, then strike it.

PRE-BEND & RELEASE: Bend the note as indicated. Strike it and release the note back to the original pitch.

UNISON BEND: Strike the two notes simultaneously and bend the lower note up to the pitch of the higher.

BEND & RESTRIKE: Strike the note and bend as indicated then restrike the string where the symbol occurs.

BEND, HOLD AND RELEASE: Same as bend and release but hold the bend for the duration of the tie.

BEND AND TAP: Bend the note as indicated and tap the higher fret while still holding the bend.

VIBRATO: The string is vibrated by rapidly bending and releasing the note with the fretting hand.

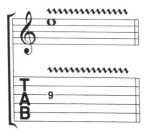

HAMMER-ON: Strike the first note with one finger, then sound the second note (on the same string) with another finger by fretting it without picking.

PULL-OFF: Place both fingers on the notes to be sounded, strike the first note and without picking, pull the finger off to sound the second note.

LEGATO SLIDE (GLISS): Strike the first note and then slide the same fret-hand finger up or down to the second note. The second note is not struck.

NOTE: The speed of any bend is indicated by the music notation and tempo.

4

SHIFT SLIDE (GLISS & RESTRIKE): Same as legato slide, except the second note is struck.

TRILL: Very rapidly alternate between the notes indicated by continuously hammering on and pulling off.

TAPPING: Hammer ("tap") the fret indicated with the pick-hand index or middle finger and pull off to the note fretted by the fret hand.

PICK SCRAPE: The edge of the pick is rubbed down (or up) the string, producing a scratchy sound.

MUFFLED STRINGS: A percussive sound is produced by laying the fret hand across the string(s) without depressing, and striking them with the pick hand.

NATURAL HARMONIC: Strike the note while the fret-hand lightly touches the string directly over the fret indicated.

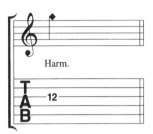

PINCH HARMONIC: The note is fretted normally and a harmonic is produced by adding the edge of the thumb or the tip of the index finger of the pick hand to the normal pick attack.

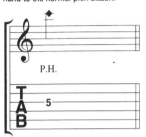

HARP HARMONIC: The note is fretted normally and a harmonic is produced by gently resting the pick hand's index finger directly above the indicated fret (in brackets) while plucking the appropriate string.

PALM MUTING: The note is partially muted by the pick hand lightly touching the string(s) just before the bridge.

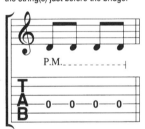

RAKE: Drag the pick across the strings indicated with a single motion.

TREMOLO PICKING: The note is picked as rapidly and continuously as possible.

ARPEGGIATE: Play the notes of the chord indicated by quickly rolling them from bottom to top.

SWEEP PICKING: Rhythmic downstroke and/or upstroke motion across the strings.

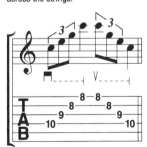

VIBRATO DIVE BAR AND RETURN: The pitch of the note or chord is dropped a specific number of steps (in rhythm) then returned to the original pitch.

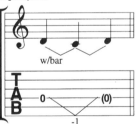

VIBRATO BAR SCOOP: Depress the bar just before striking the note, then quickly release the bar.

VIBRATO BAR DIP: Strike the note and then immediately drop a specific number of steps, then release back to the original pitch.

additional musical definitions

(accent) • Accentuate note (play it louder).

(accent) • Accentuate note with great intensity.

(staccato) • Shorten time value of note.

⊓ • Downstroke

∨ • Upstroke

NOTE: Tablature numbers in brackets mean:
1. The note is sustained, but a new articulation (such as hammer on or slide) begins.
2. A note may be fretted but not necessarily played.

D.%. al Coda

D.C. al Fine

tacet

• Go back to the sign (%), then play until the bar marked *To Coda* ⊕ then skip to the section marked ⊕ *Coda*.

• Go back to the beginning of the song and play until the bar marked *Fine*.

• Instrument is silent (drops out).

• Repeat bars between signs.

• When a repeated section has different endings, play the first ending only the first time and the second ending only the second time.

Across The Universe

Words & Music by John Lennon & Paul McCartney

Intro

2 bar count in:

* optional bass

sim.

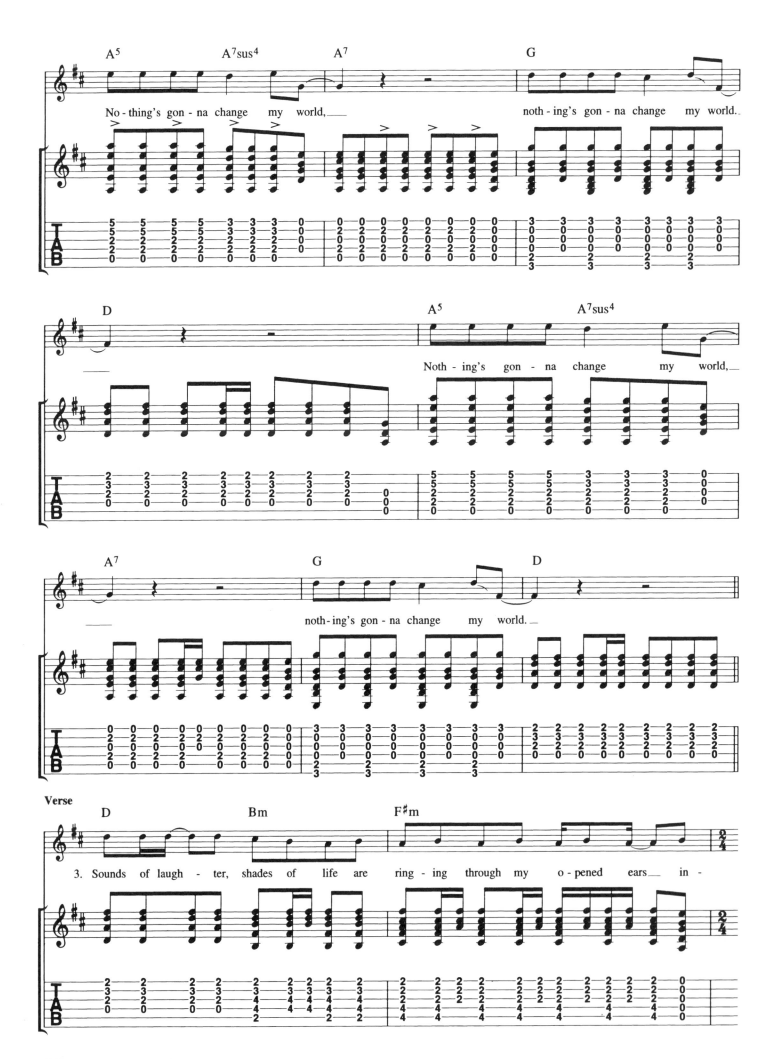

Angels

Words & Music by Robbie Williams & Guy Chambers

when I come to call she won't for-sake

me, I'm lov-ing an-gels in-stead.

Solo

w/slide

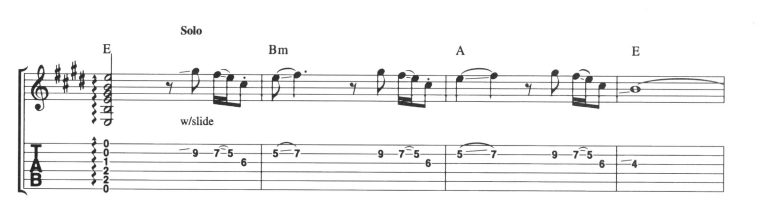

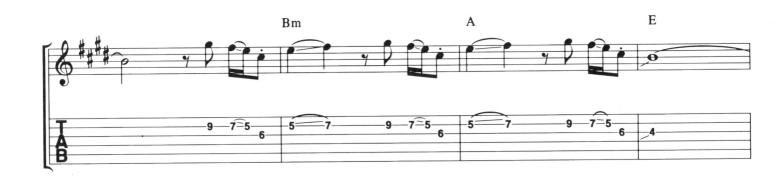

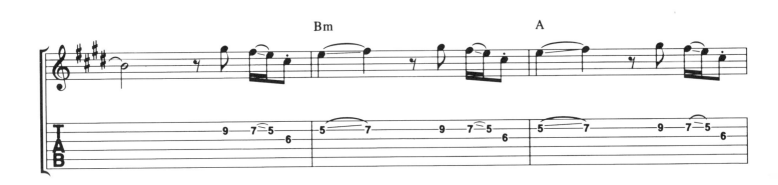

Chorus

And through it all_____ she of - fers me__ pro - tec -

w/clean tone

- tion,__ a lot of love and af - fec - tion wheth-er I'm right or

Babylon

Words & Music by David Gray

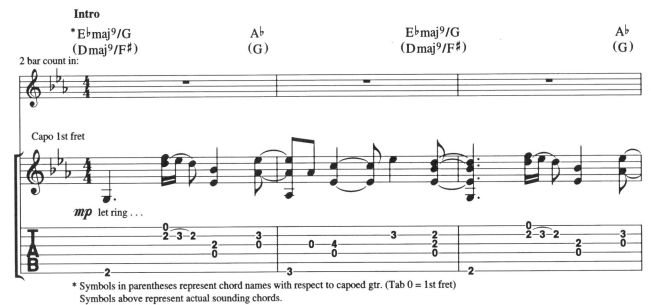

* Symbols in parentheses represent chord names with respect to capoed gtr. (Tab 0 = 1st fret)
Symbols above represent actual sounding chords.

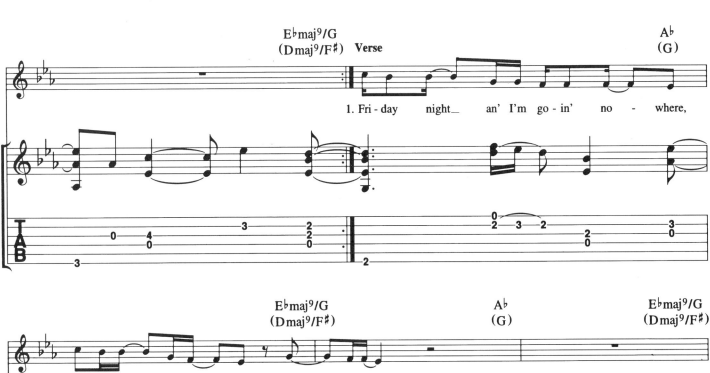

Fields Of Gold

Words & Music by Sting

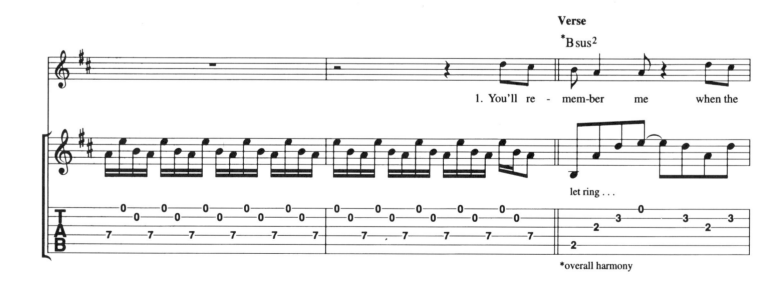

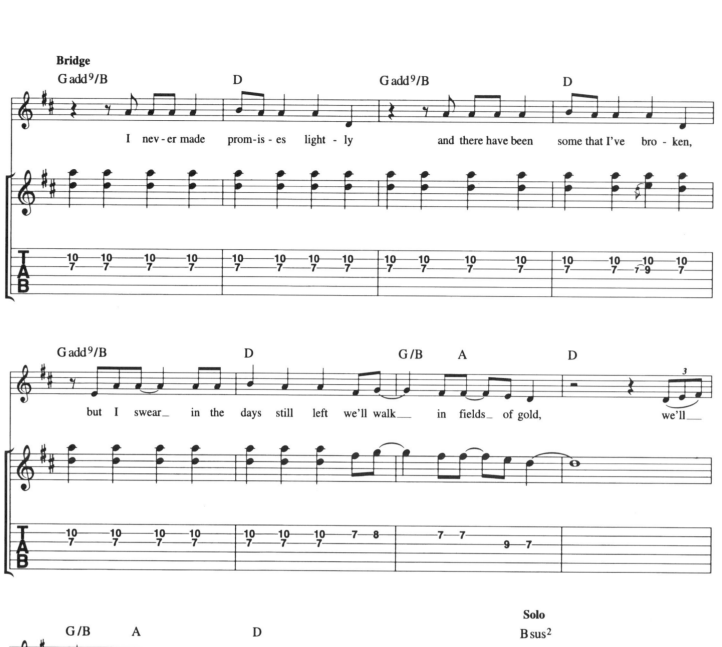

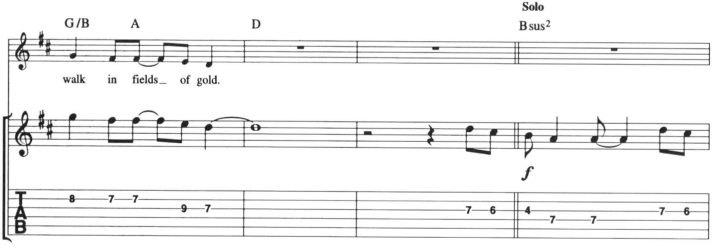

Guitar Man

Words & Music By Jerry Reed

By sun-down I'd____ left Kings - ton with my

So I bought me a ride____ down to Ma - con, Georg - ia on an

- bile. Make it on out to a club called Jack's if you

G⁷

gui - tar un - der my coat.____ I hitch - hiked all____ the way down__ to Mem -

over - loaded poul - try . truck.____ I thumbed on down to Pan - a - ma Ci -

got a little time to kill.____ An', just fol - low that__ crowd__ of peo -

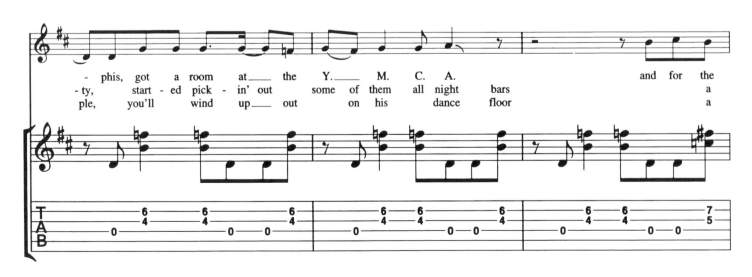

- phis, got a room at____ the Y.____ M. C. A. and for the

- ty, start - ed pick - in' out some of them all night bars a

ple, you'll wind up__ out on his dance floor a

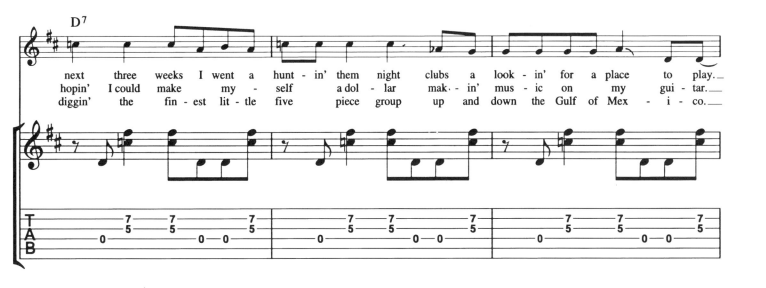

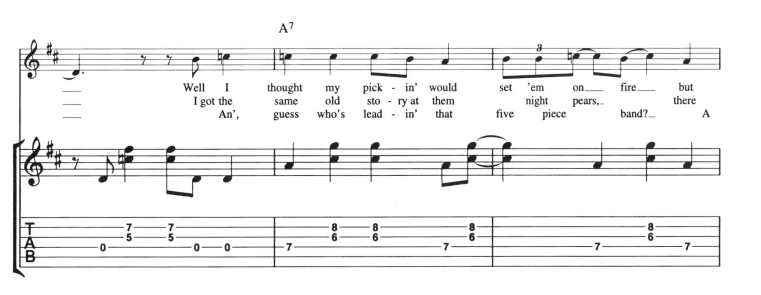

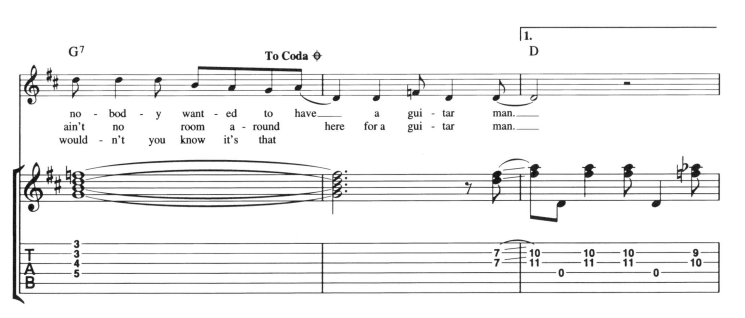

38

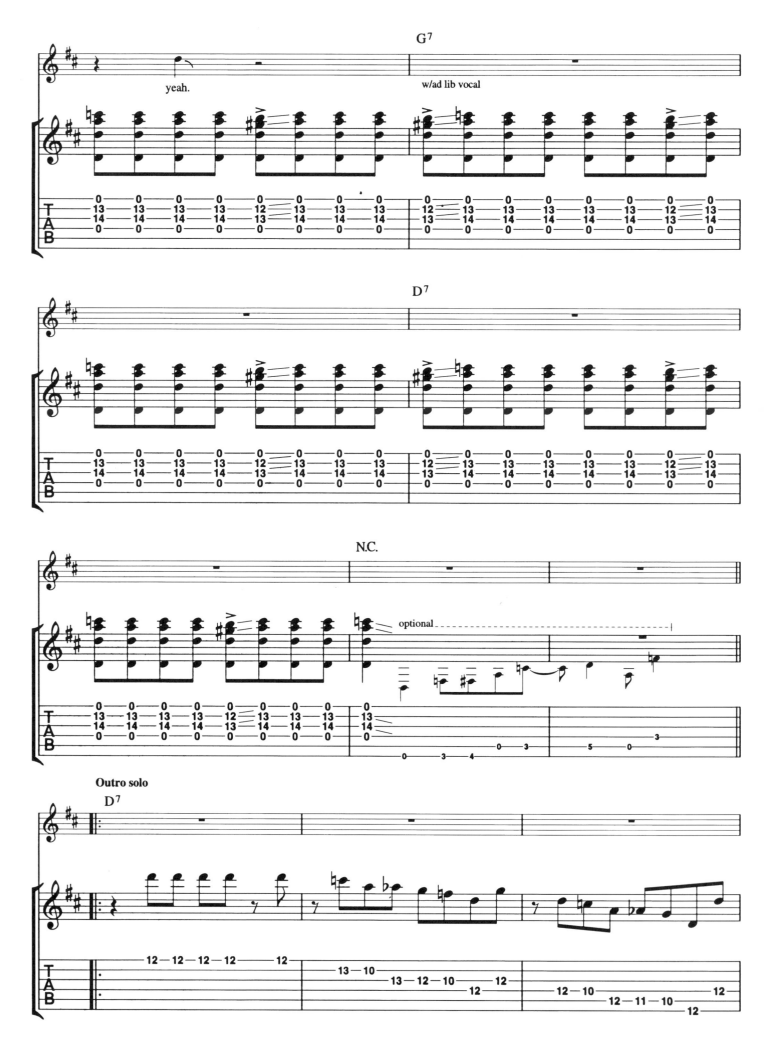

Have You Ever Really Loved A Woman?

Words & Music by Bryan Adams, Robert John Lange & Michael Kamen

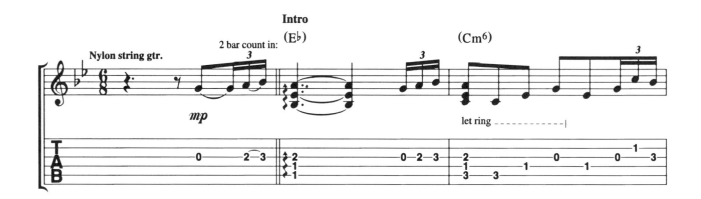

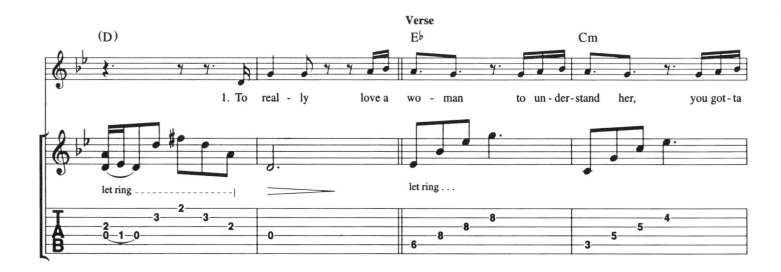

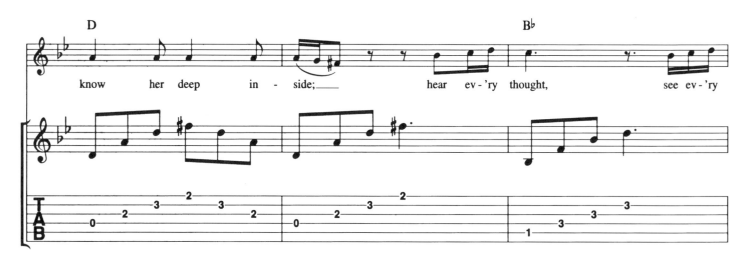

45

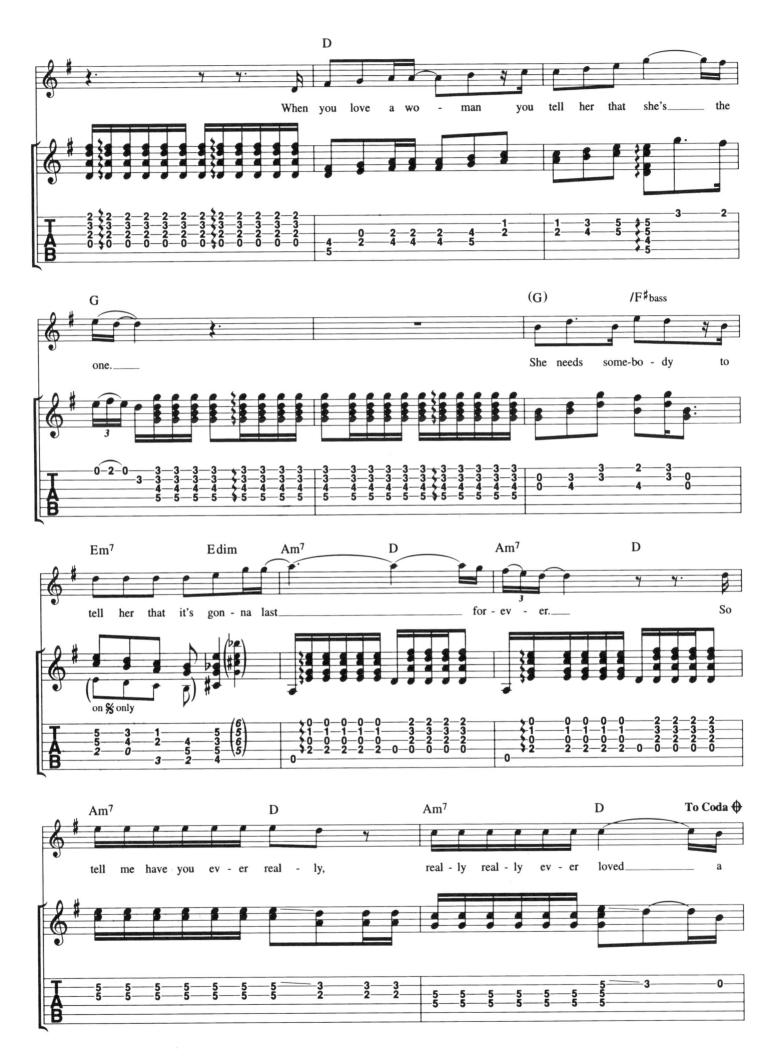

47

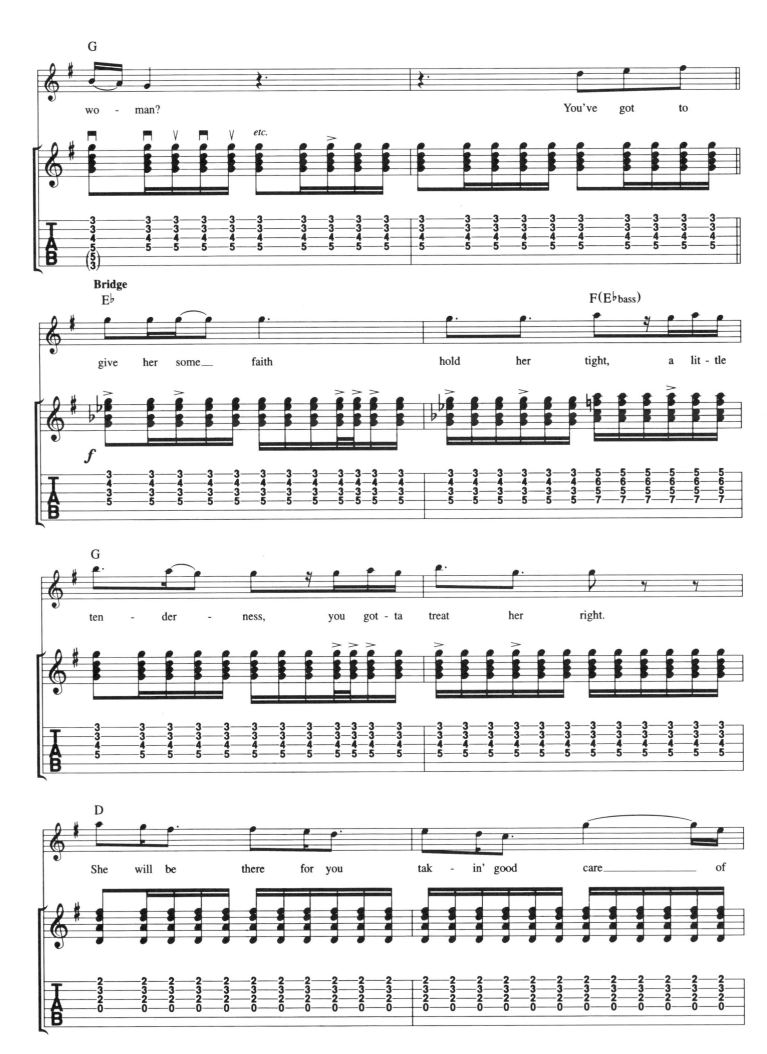

(You really gotta love your woman, yeah.)

Solo

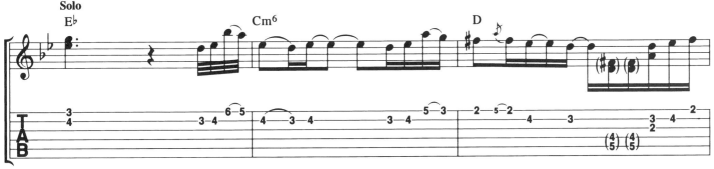

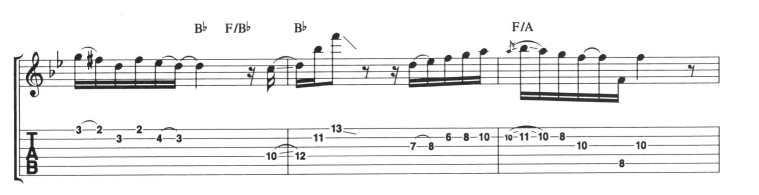

Then when you

A Hazy Shade Of Winter

Words & Music by Paul Simon

* Symbols in parentheses represent chord names with respect to capoed gtr. (Tab 0 = 5th fret)
Symbols above represent actual sounding chords.

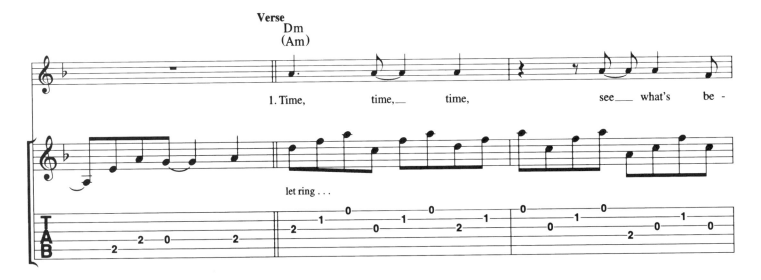

Lay Lady Lay

Words & Music by Bob Dylan

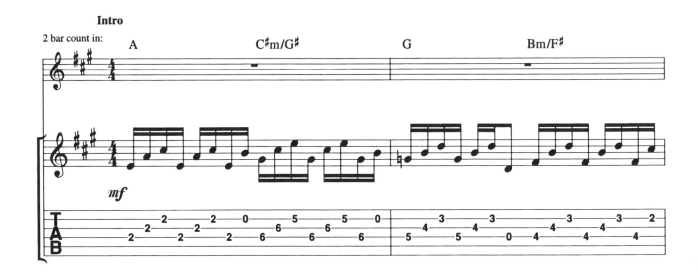

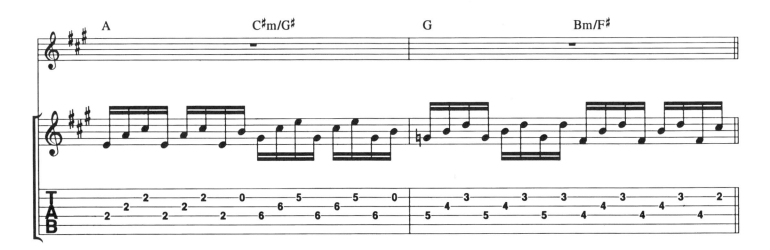

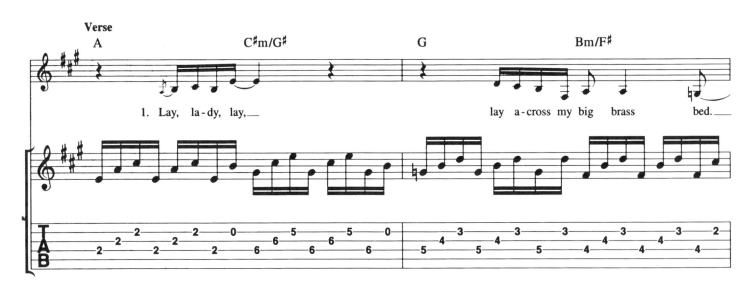

Layla

Words & Music by Eric Clapton & Jim Gordon

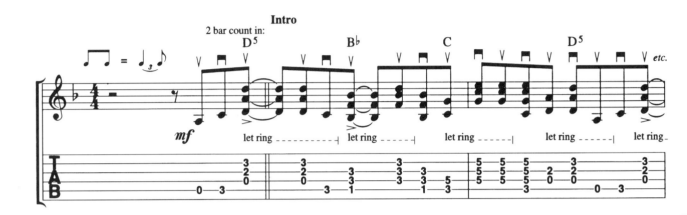

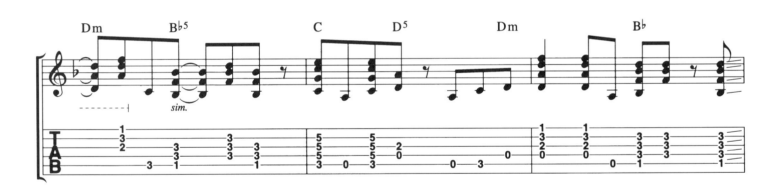

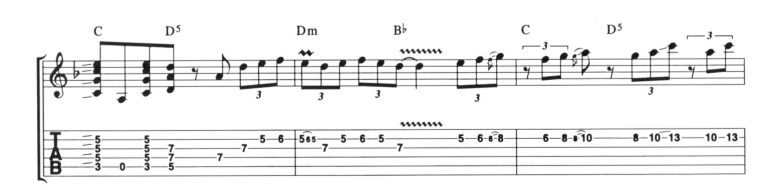

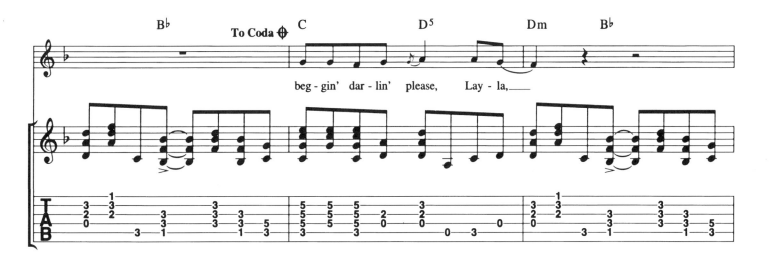

beg - gin' dar - lin' please, Lay - la,___

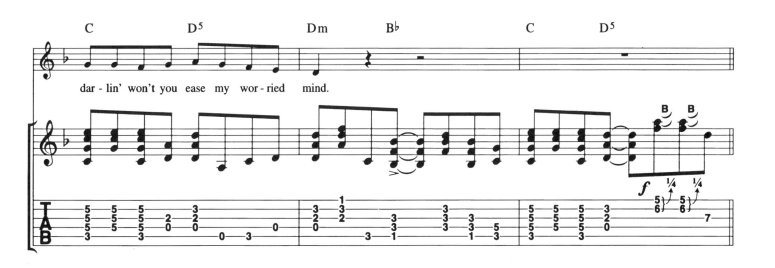

dar - lin' won't you ease my wor - ried mind.

Solo

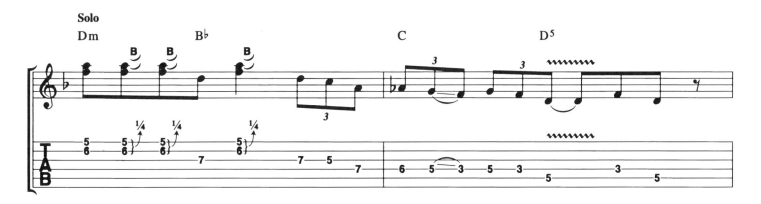

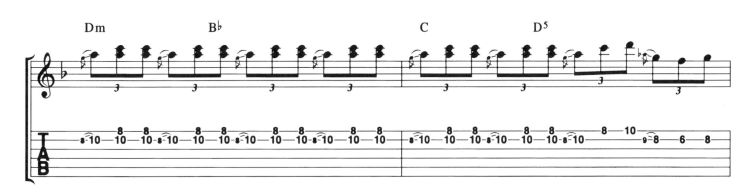

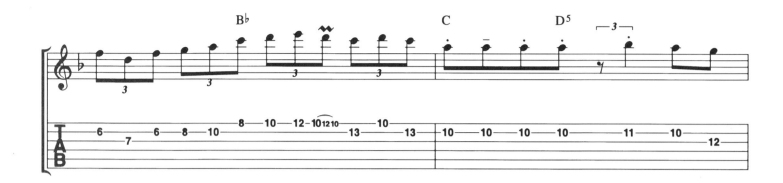

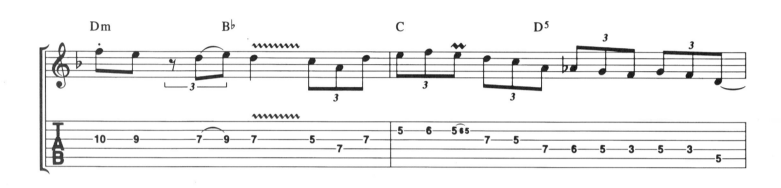

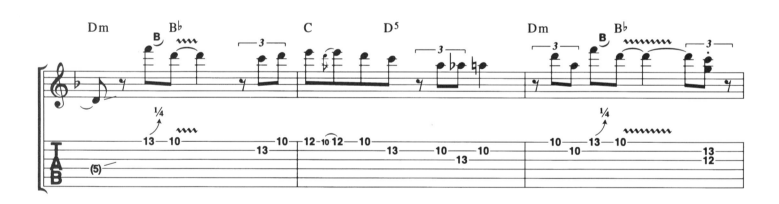

Maria Maria

Words & Music by Wyclef Jean, Jerry Duplessis & Carlos Santana

The Man Who Sold The World

Words & Music by David Bowie

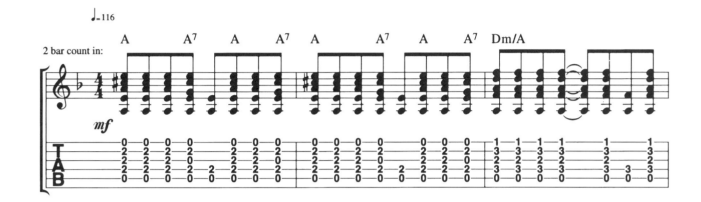

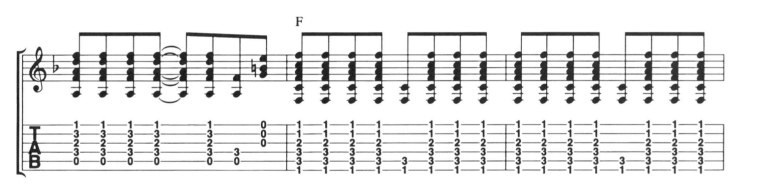

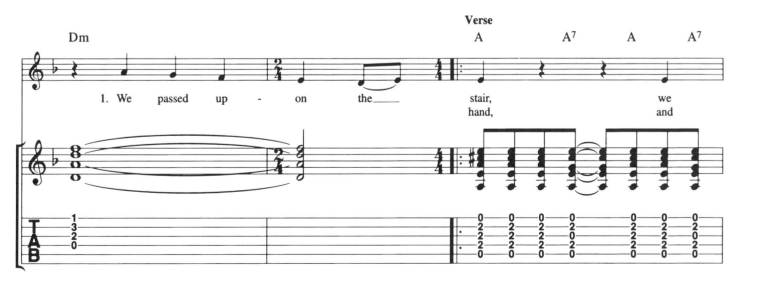

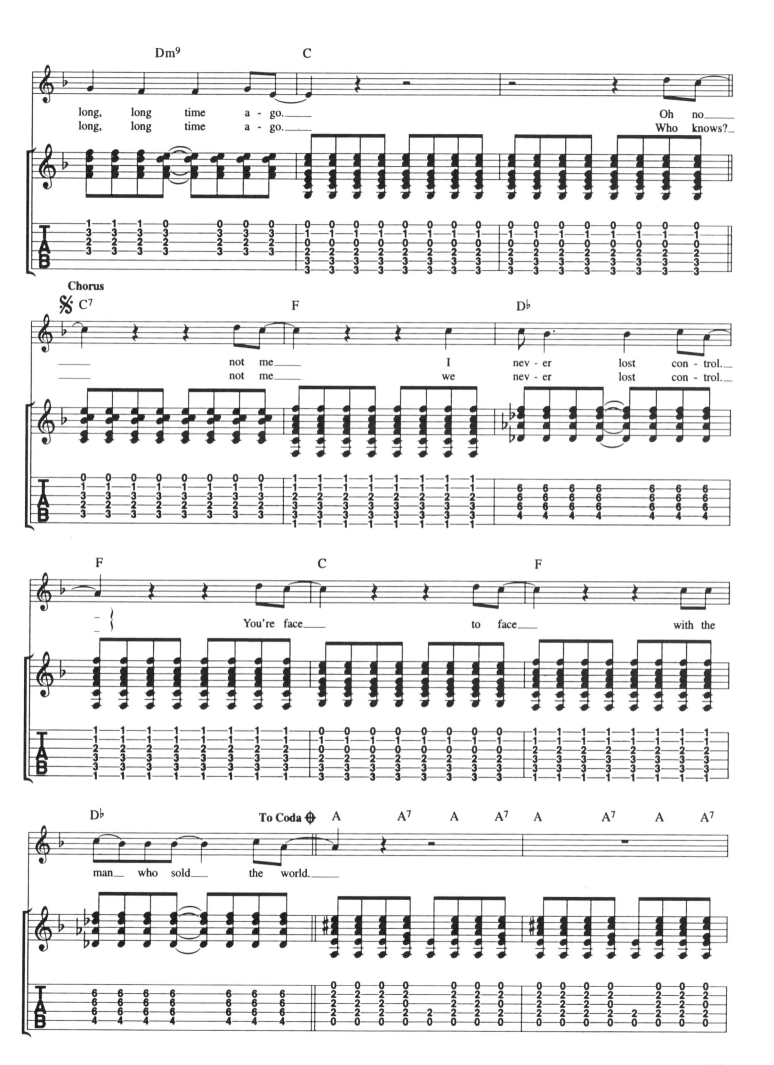

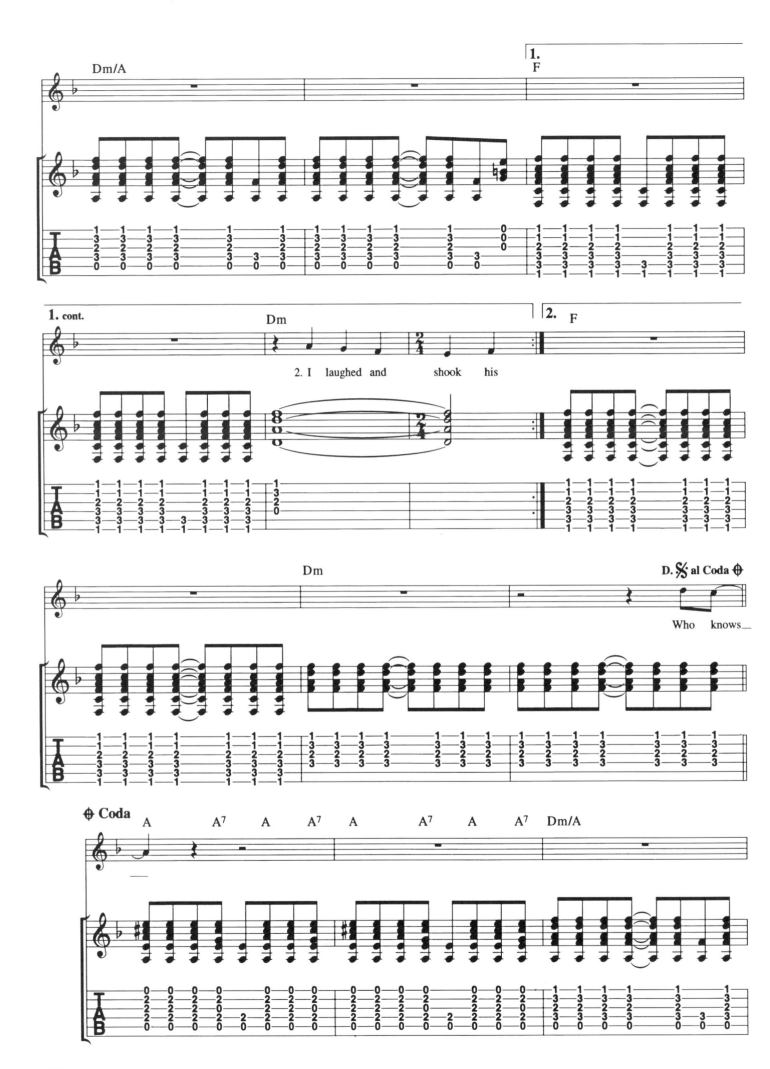

2. I laughed and shook his

Who knows

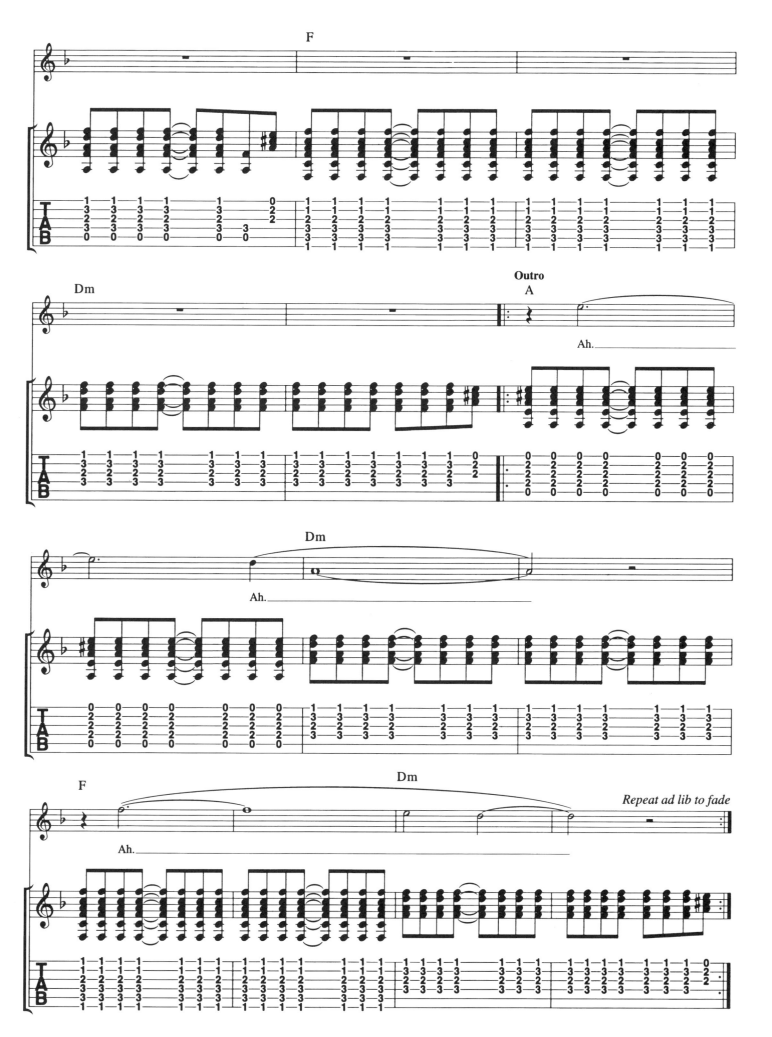

Me And Julio Down By The Schoolyard

Words & Music by Paul Simon

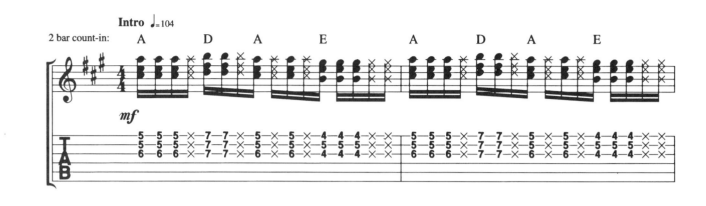

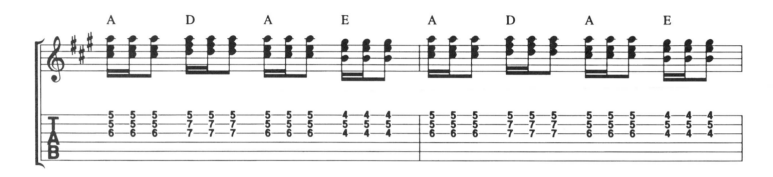

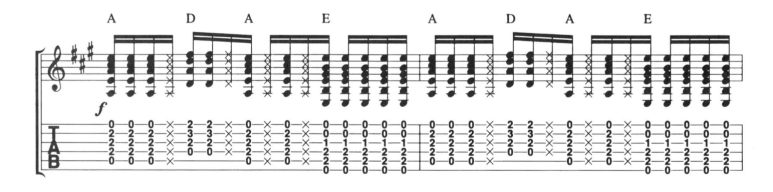

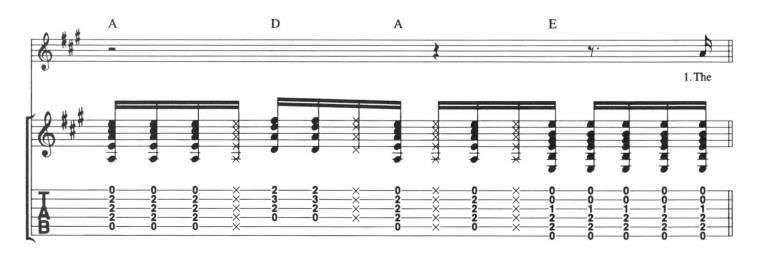

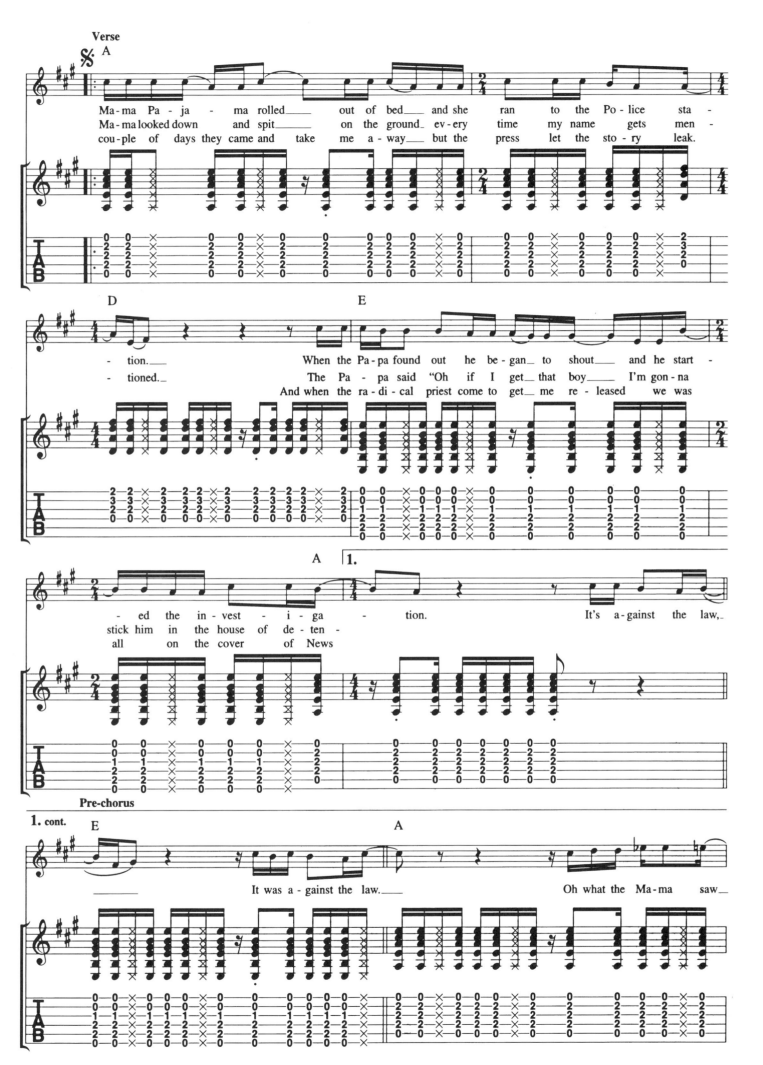

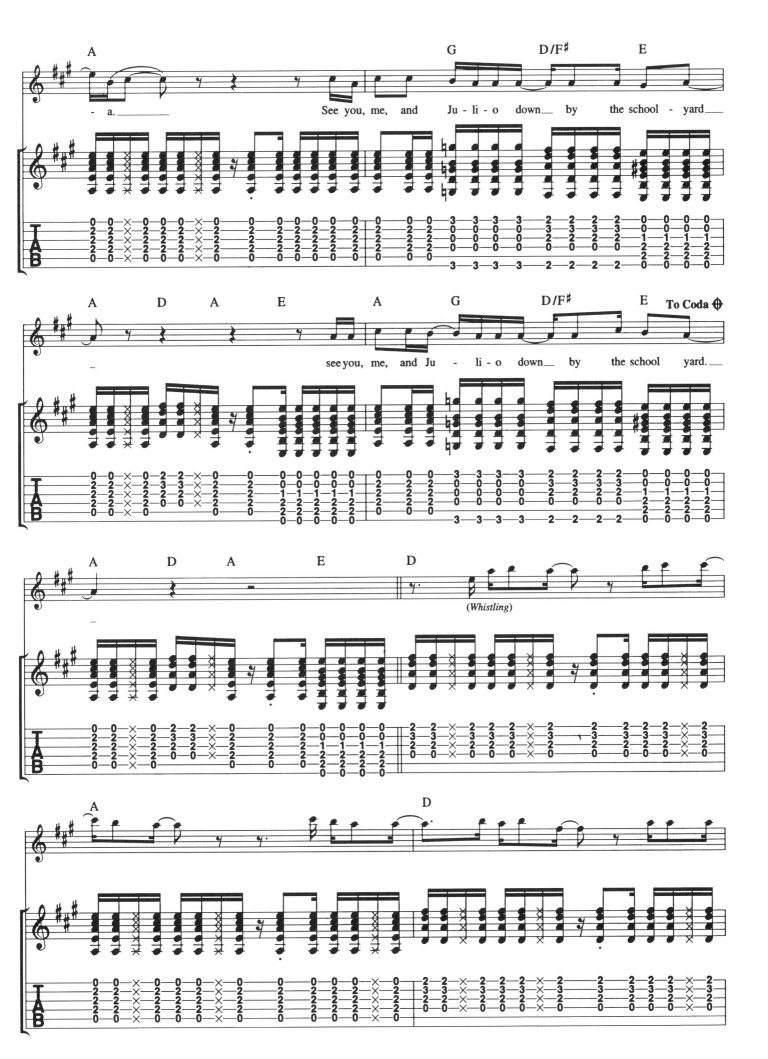

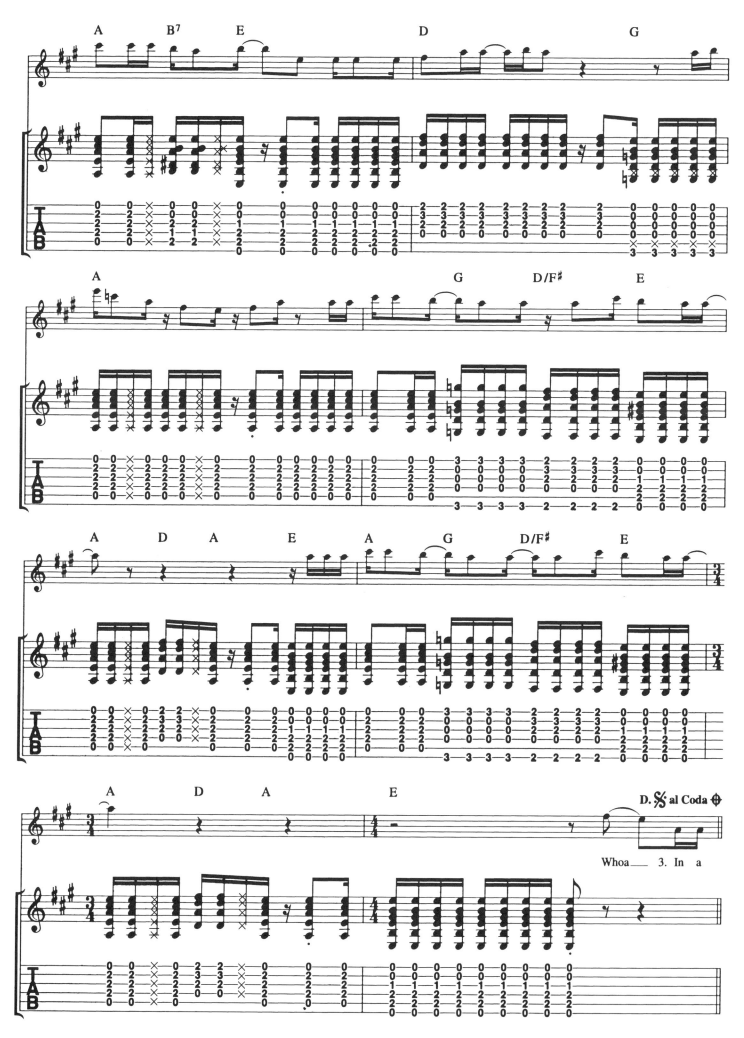

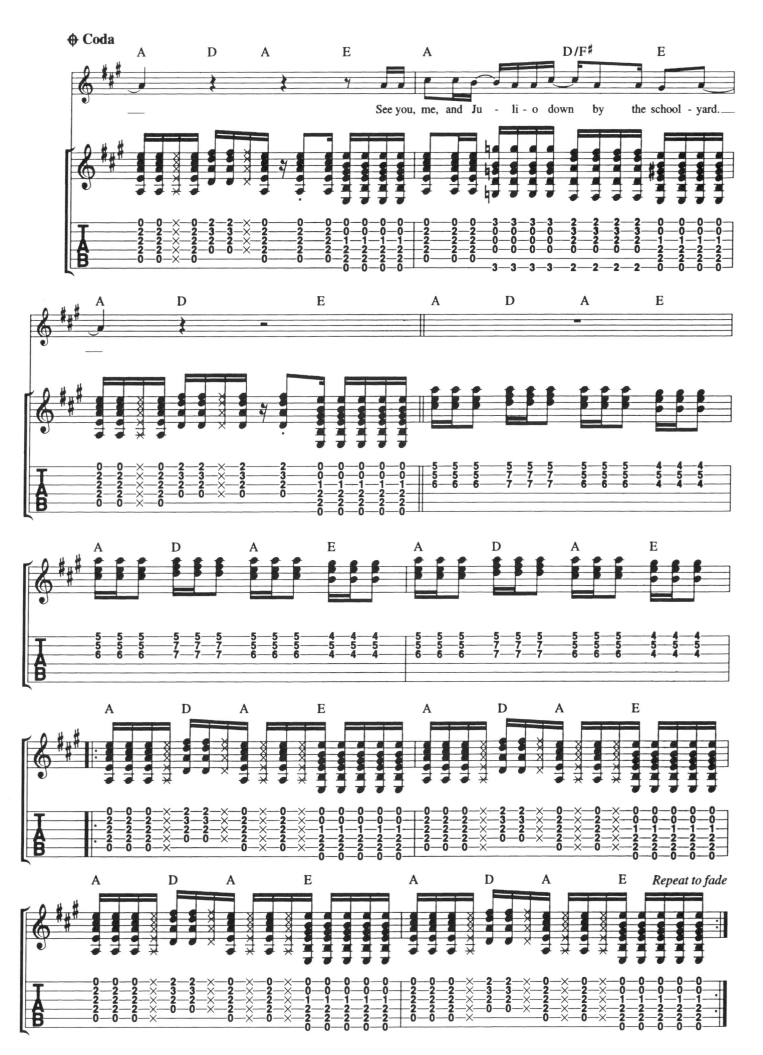

Not Fade Away

Words & Music by Charles Hardin & Norman Petty

Intro

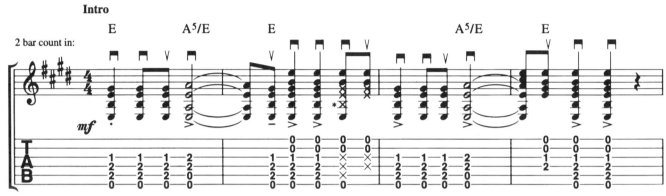

* ✕ = release fretted string to give percussive feel

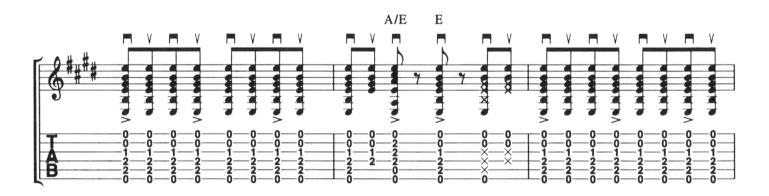

Verse

1. I wan - na tell you how it's_____ gon - na be,
2. My love's big - ger than a Cad - il - lac,
3.(%) I'm gon - na tell you how it's_____ gon - na be,

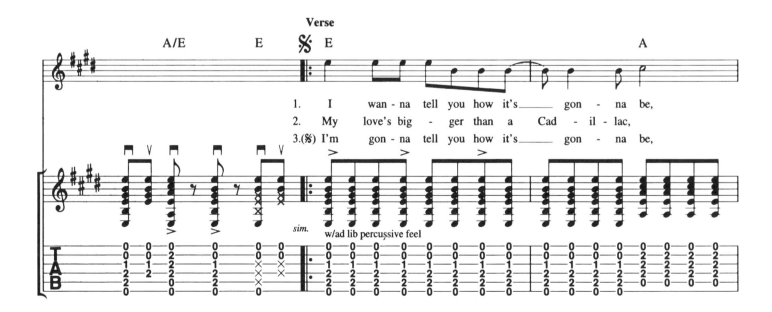

sim.

w/ad lib percussive feel

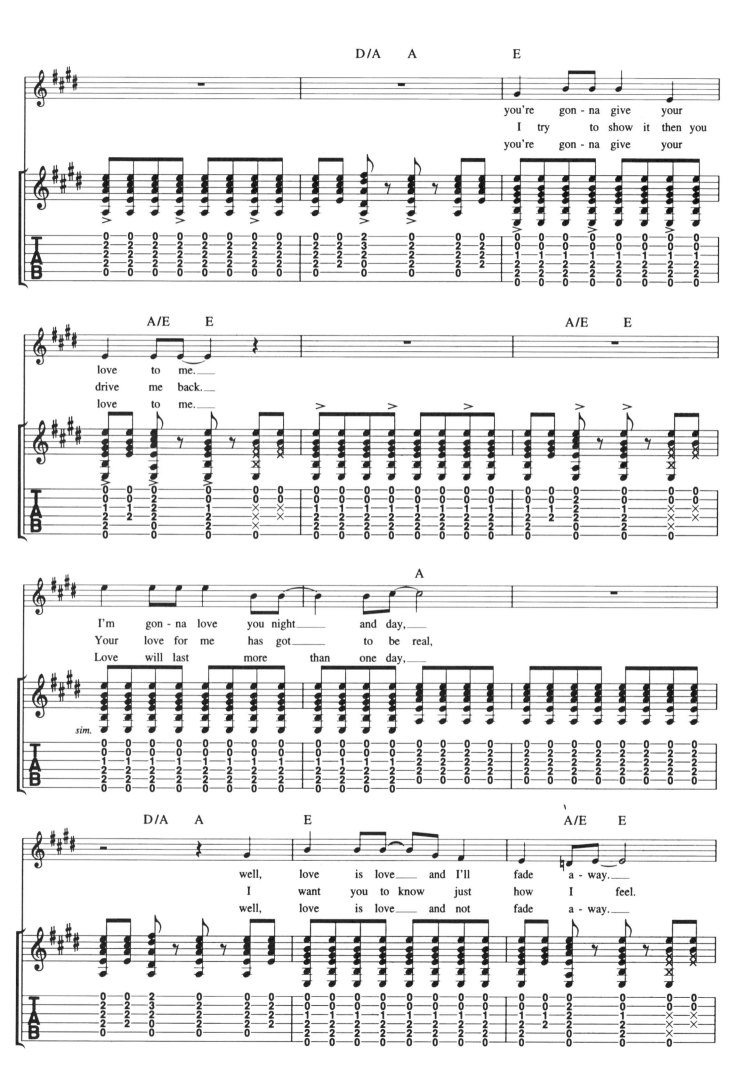

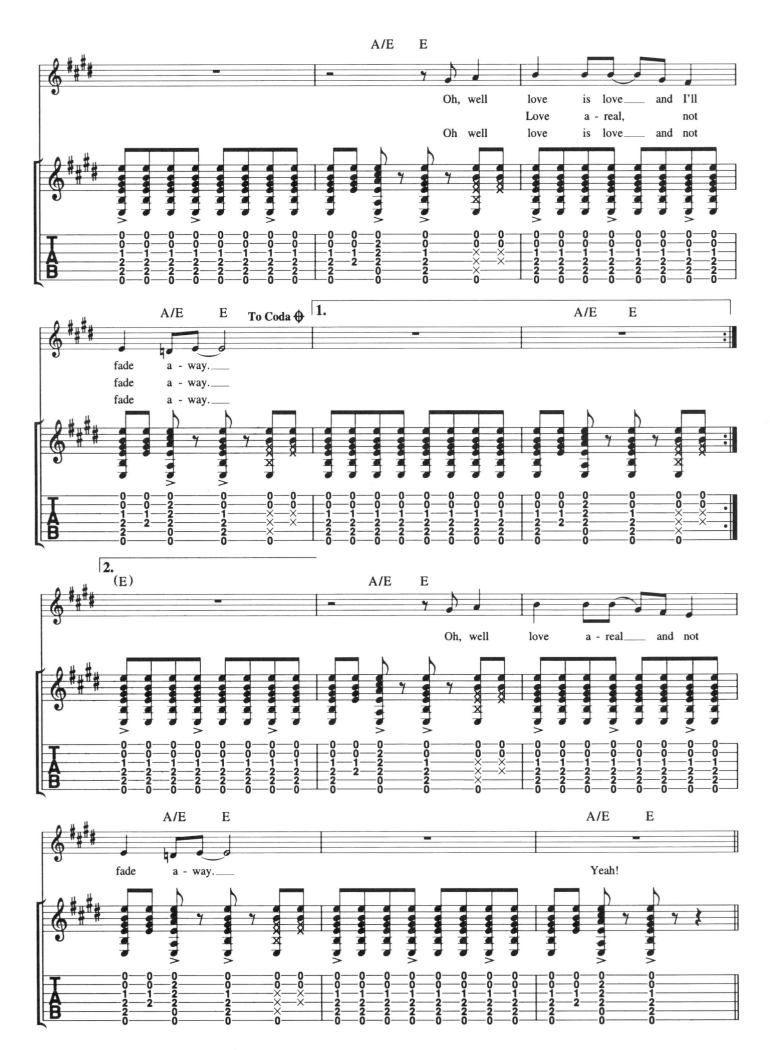

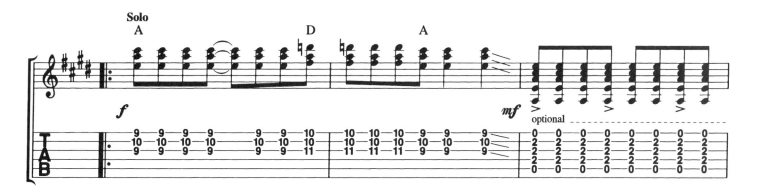

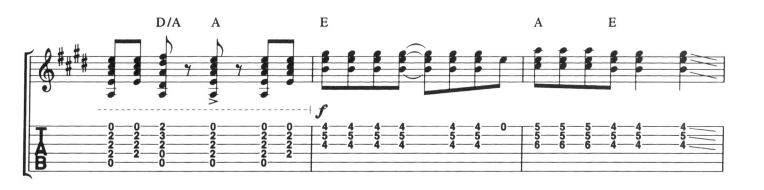

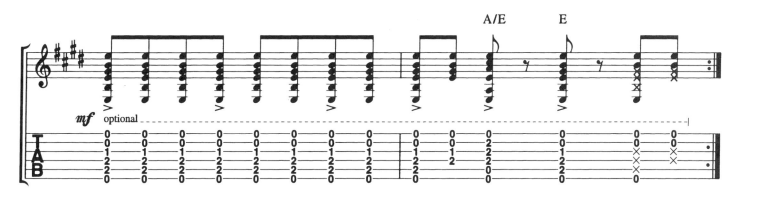

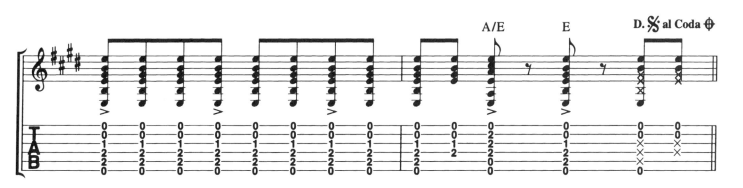

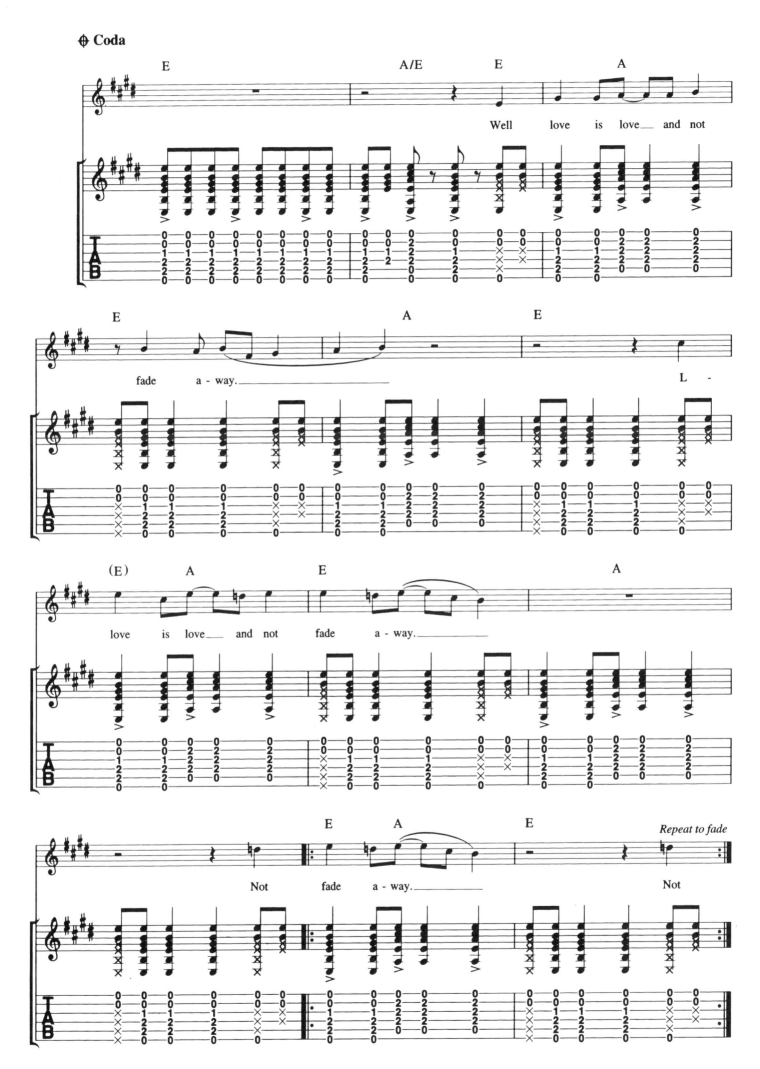

Nothing Else Matters

Words & Music by James Hetfield & Lars Ulrich

2 bar count in

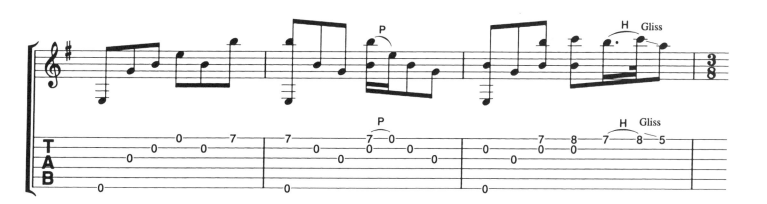

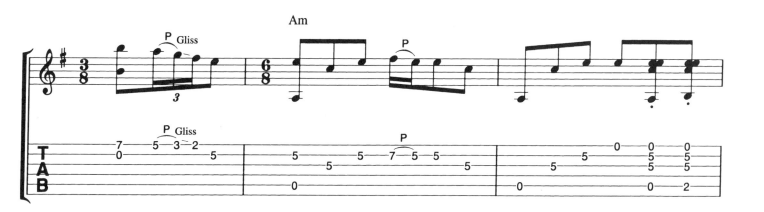

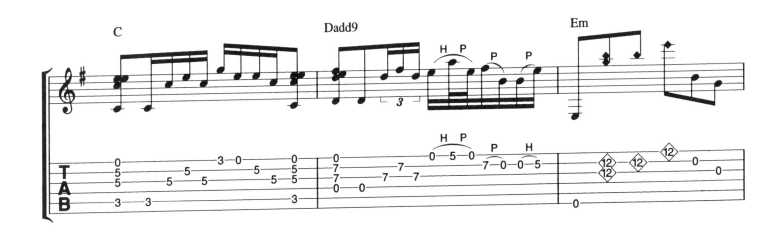

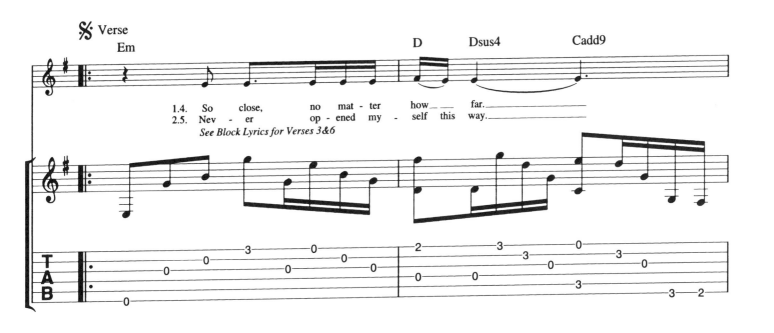

𝄋 Verse

1.4. So close, no mat-ter how___ far.___

2.5. Nev - er op - ened my - self this way.___

See Block Lyrics for Verses 3&6

Could - n't be much more___ from the heart.___

Life is ours we live it our way.

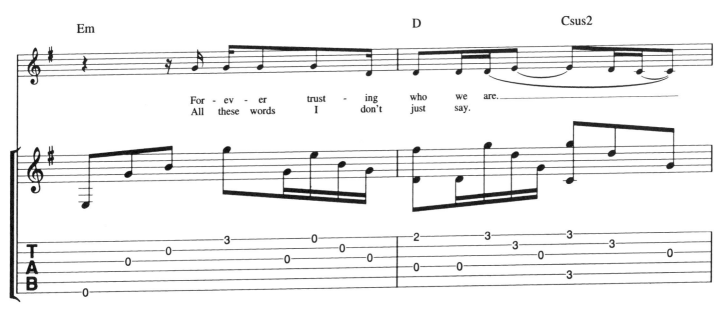

For - ev - er trust - ing who we are.___

All these words I don't just who we say.

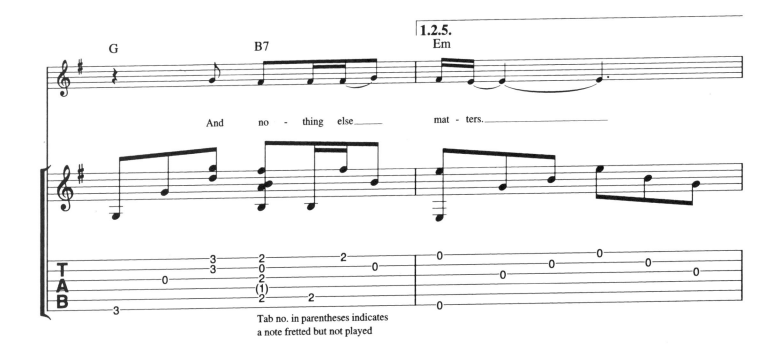

Tab no. in parentheses indicates
a note fretted but not played

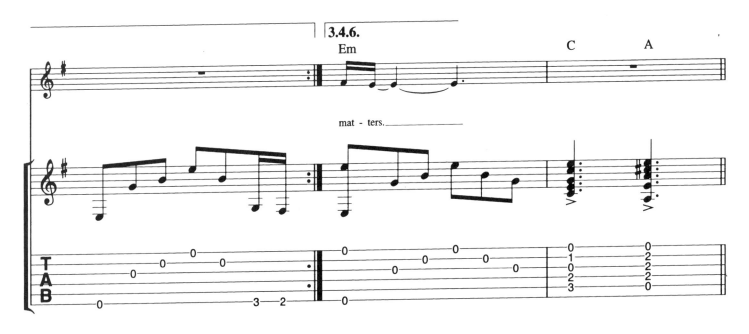

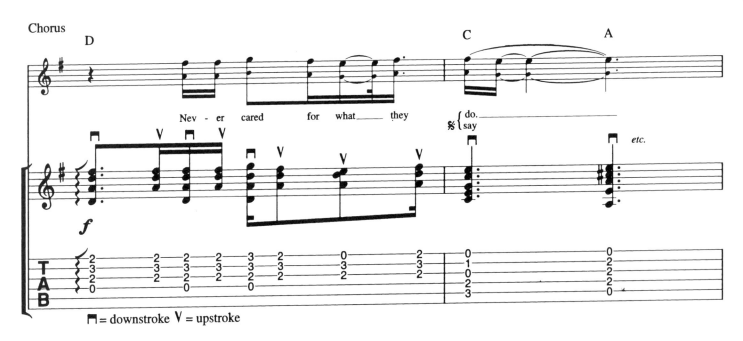

⊓ = downstroke V = upstroke

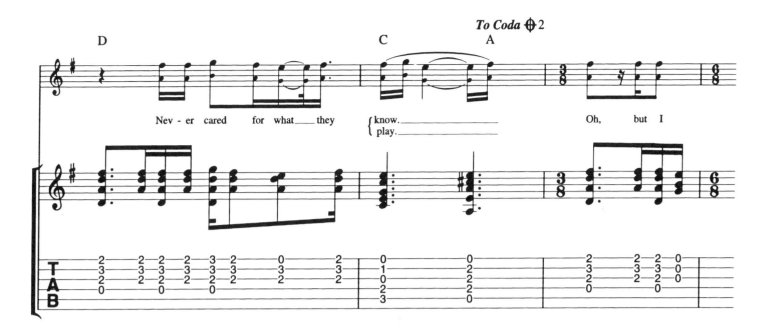

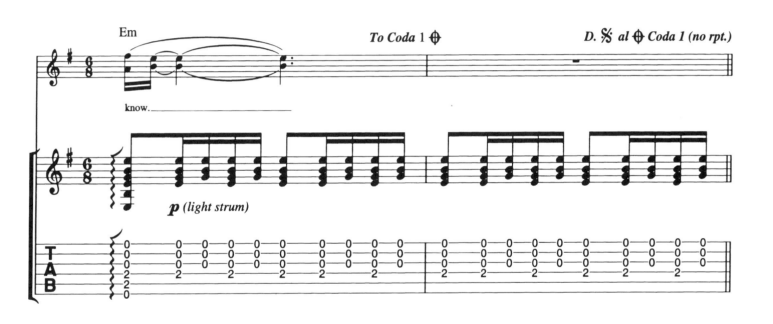

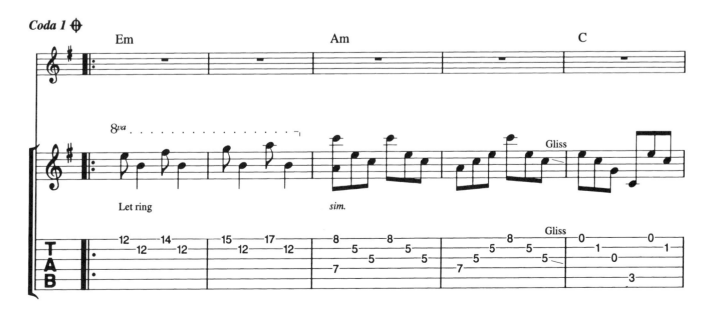

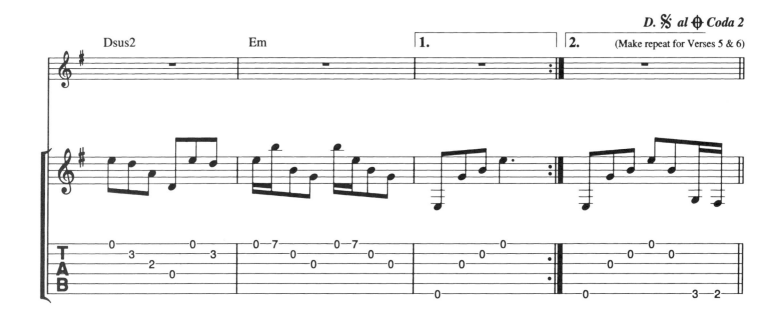

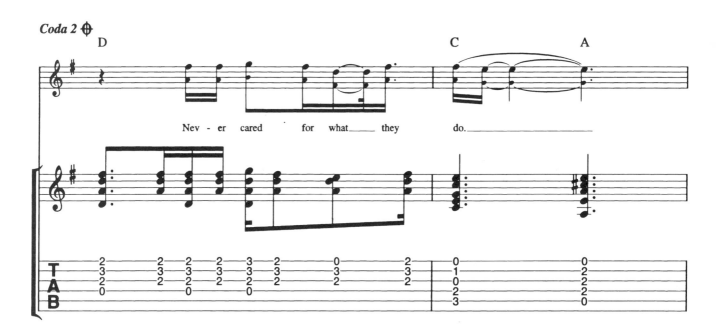

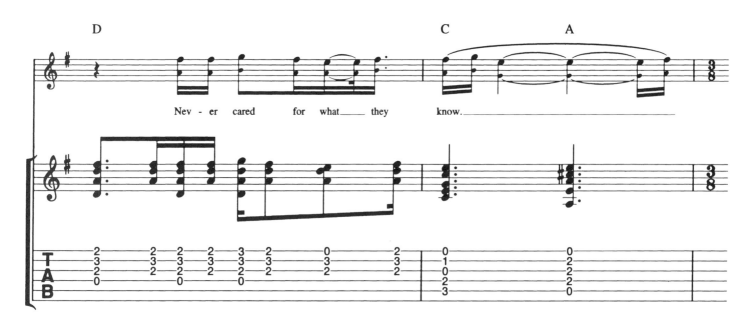

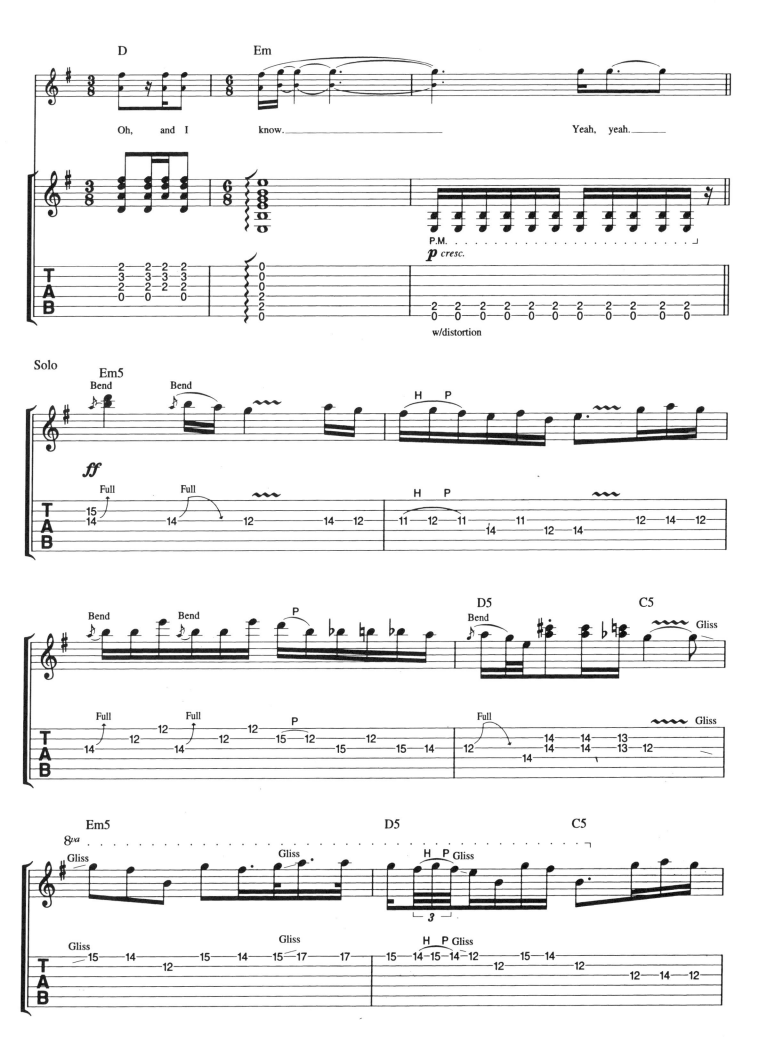

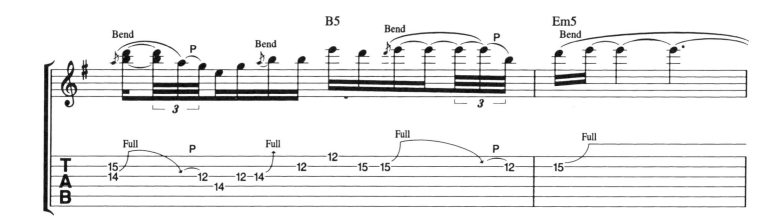

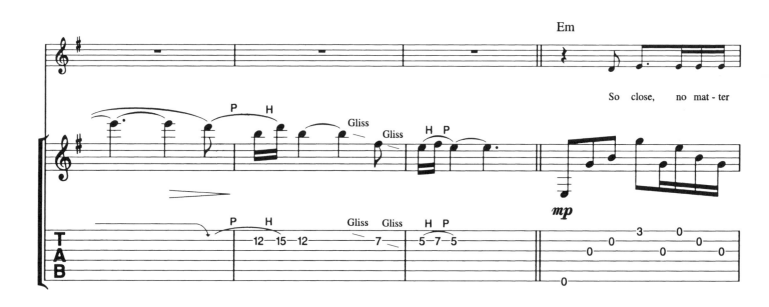

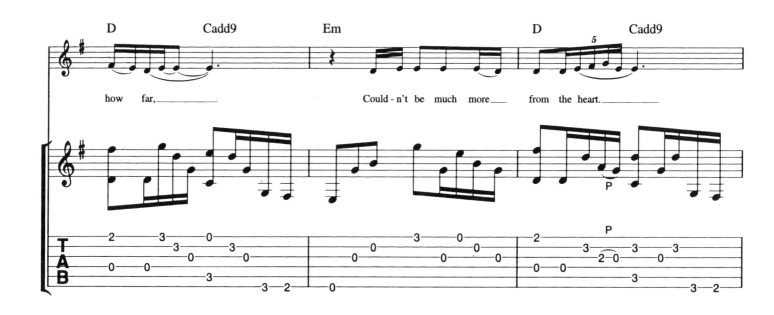

106

For - ev - er trust - ing who we are._____ No, noth - ing else_____

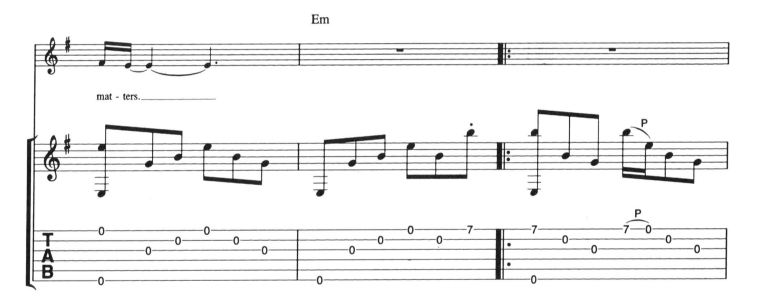

mat - ters._____

Repeat to fade

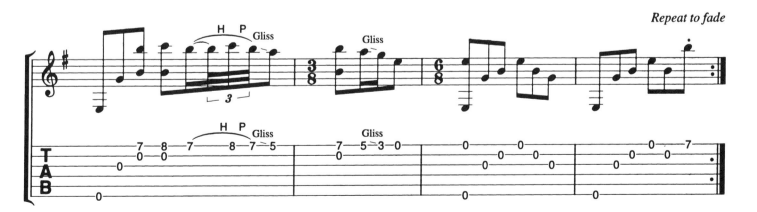

Verse 3 & 6   Trust I seek and I find in you
Ev'ryday for us something new
Open mind for a diff'rent view
And nothing else matters.

Pinball Wizard

Words & Music by Pete Townshend

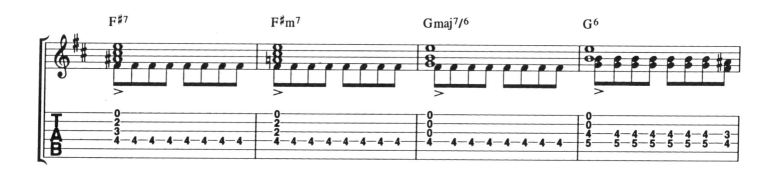

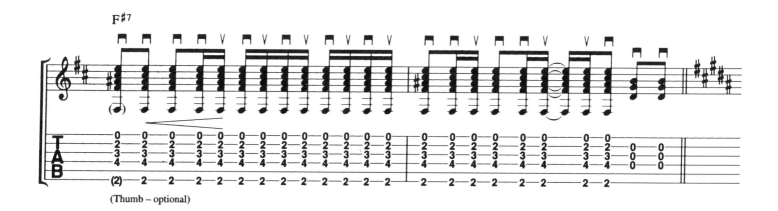

(Thumb – optional)

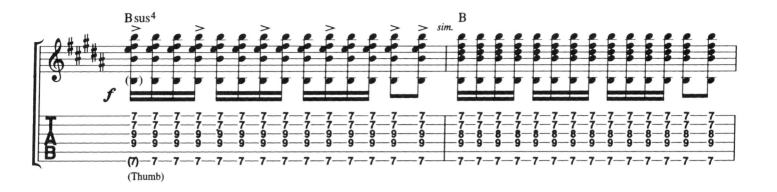

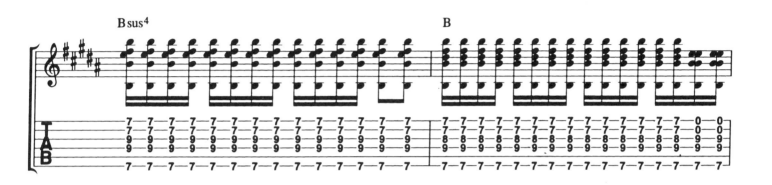

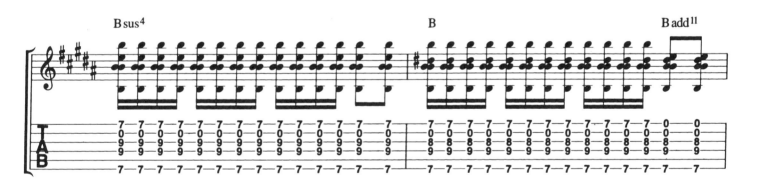

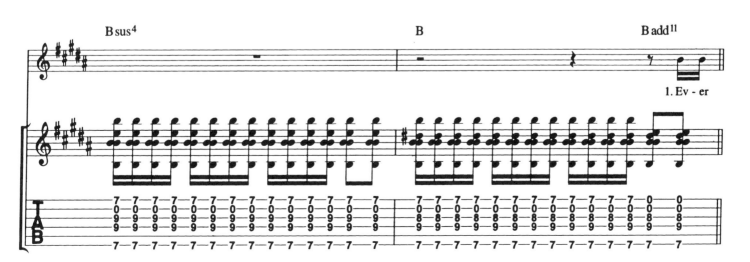

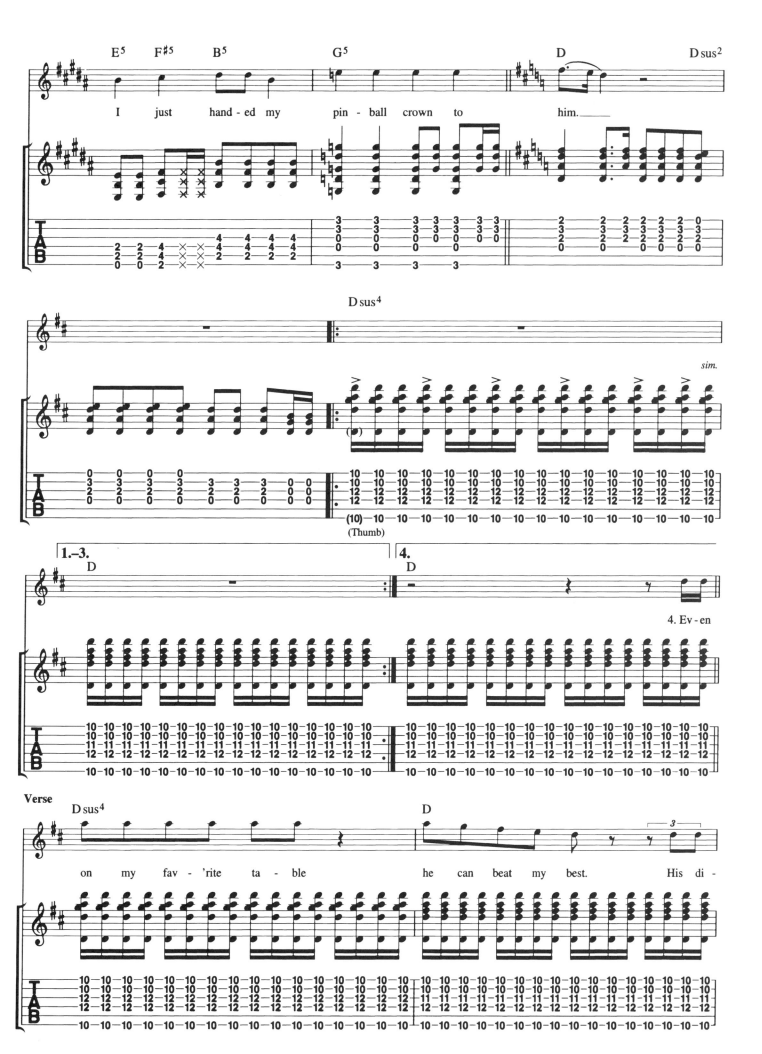

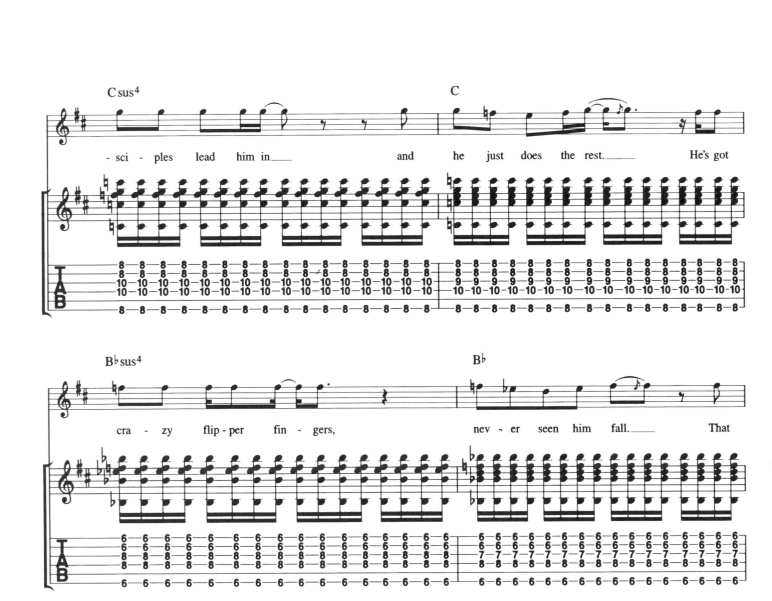

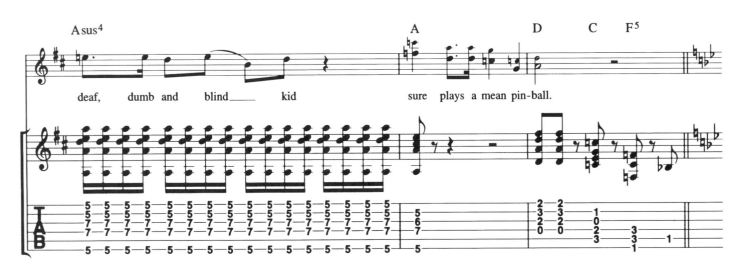

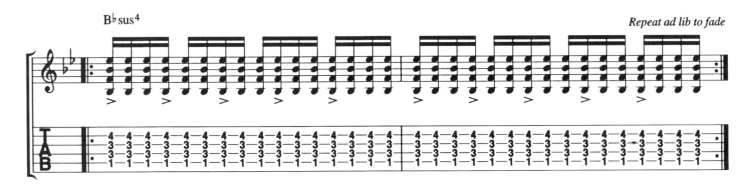

116

Spanish Caravan

Words & Music by Jim Morrison, Robbie Krieger, Ray Manzarek & John Densmore

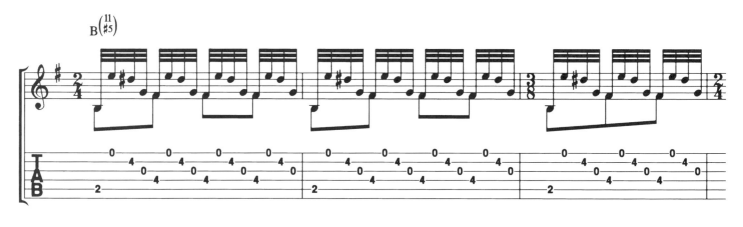

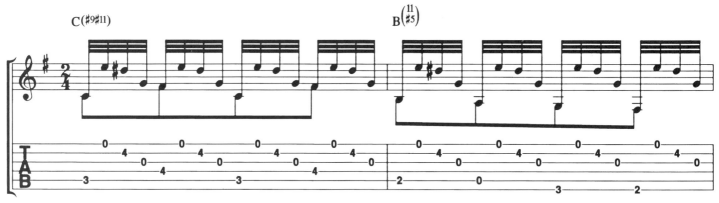

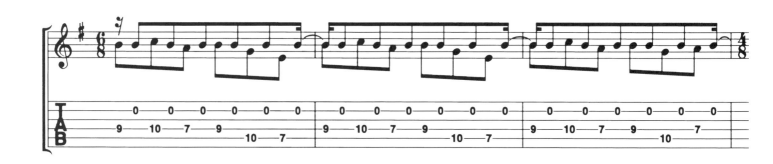

118

Take me   Span - ish   car - a - van,_____   yes   I

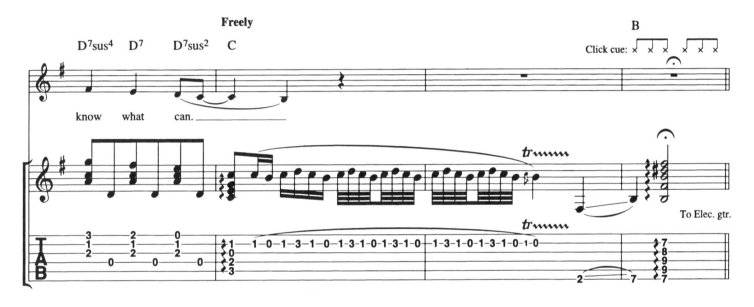

know   what   can._____

To Elec. gtr.

w/distortion & fuzz

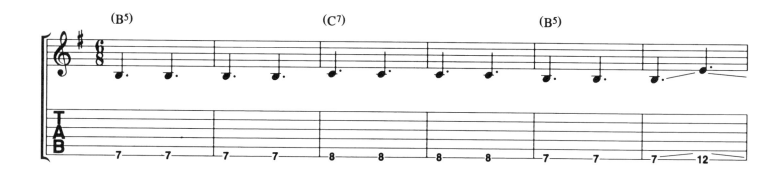

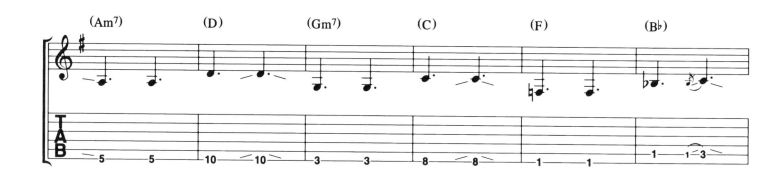

Verse

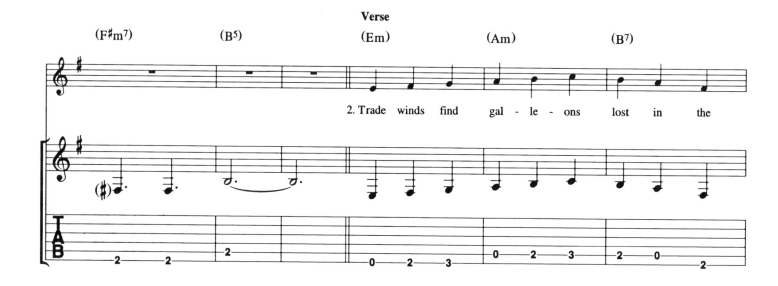

2. Trade winds find gal - le - ons lost in the

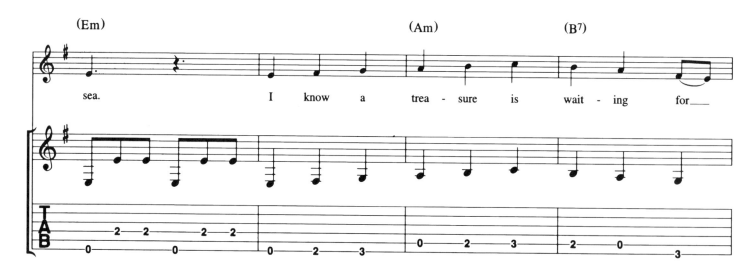

sea. I know a trea - sure is wait - ing for___

Romeo And Juliet

Words & Music by Mark Knopfler

* Gtr. tuned to F B♭ F B♭ D F

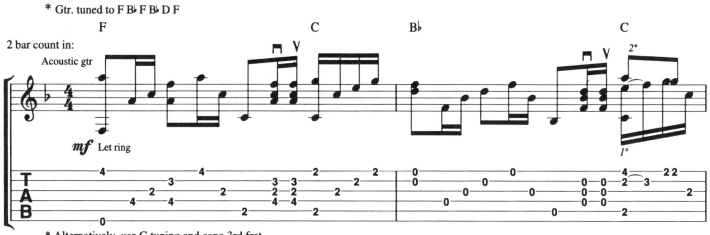

* Alternatively, use G tuning and capo 3rd fret

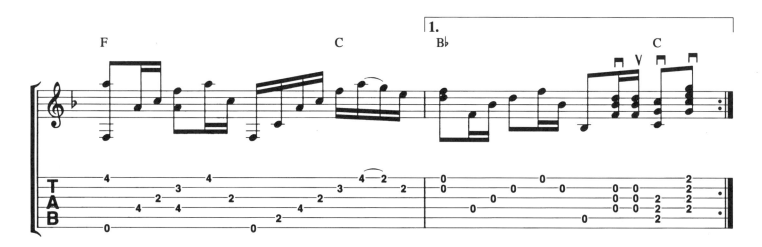

1. A love struck Ro - me - o   sings a street-suss se - re - nade,
(See block lyrics for Verses 2 & 3)

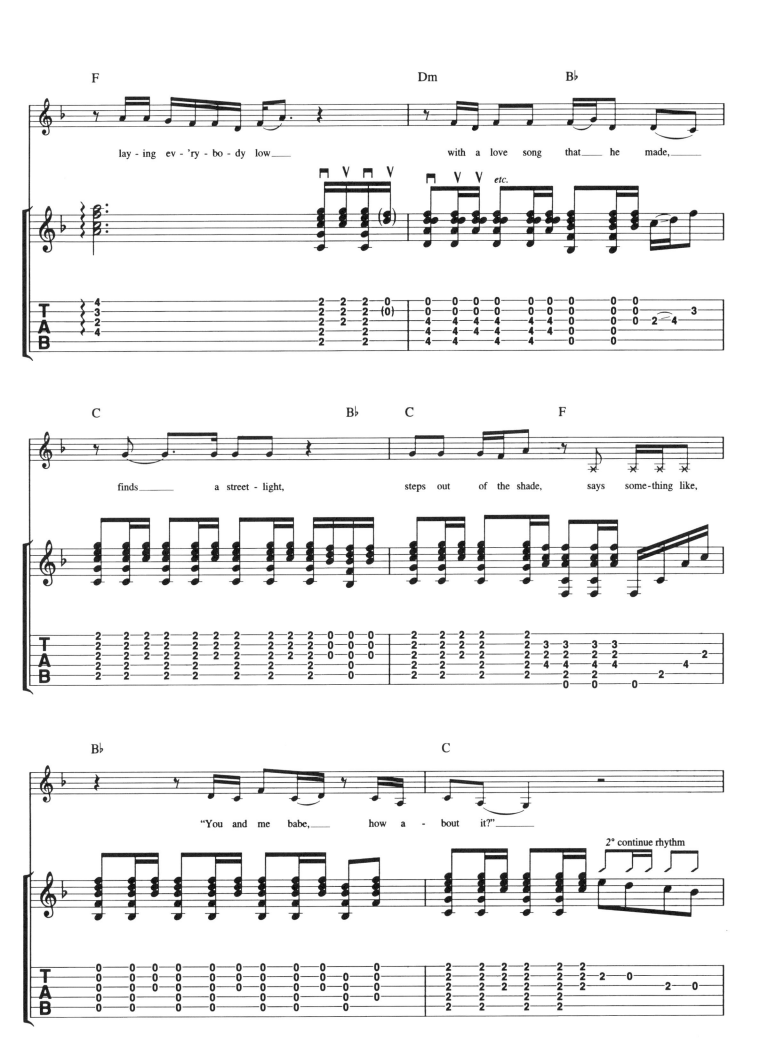

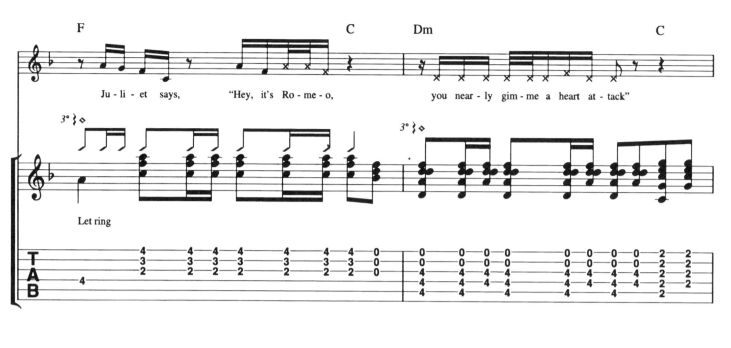

Ju - li - et says, "Hey, it's Ro - me - o, you near - ly gim - me a heart at - tack"

Let ring

He's un - der - neath the win - dow, she's sing - ing "Hey la, my boy - friend's back,

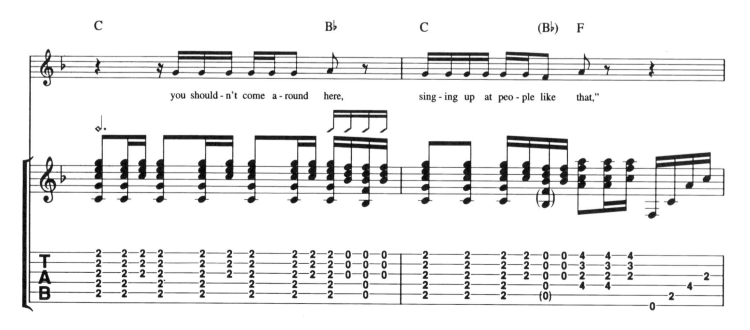

you should - n't come a - round here, sing - ing up at peo - ple like that,"

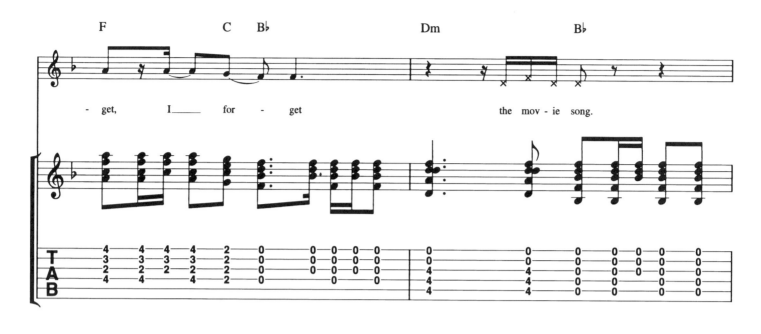

- get, I___ for - get   the mov - ie song.

When___ you gon - na re - a - lise   it was   just   that the time   was wrong,___

Ju - li - et?___

lay - ing ev - 'ry - bo - dy low,___ with a love song that___ he made,___

finds a con - ve - ni - ent street light steps out of the shade,___ he says some - thing like,

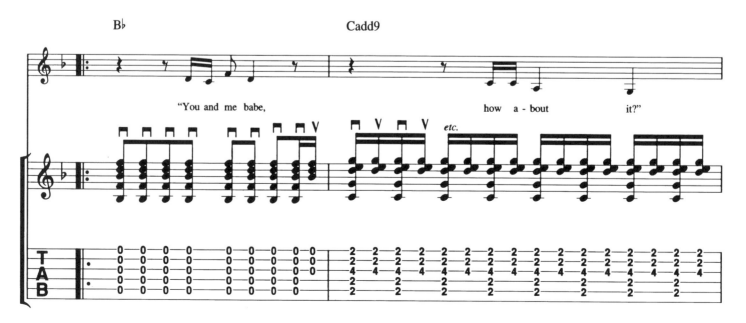

"You and me babe, how a - bout it?"

130

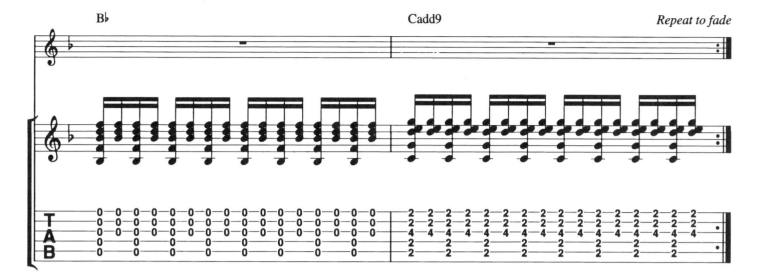

Verse 2:	Came up on different streets They both were streets of shame Both dirty, both mean Yes and the dream was just the same And I dreamed your dream for you And now your dream is real How can you look at me as if I was Just another one of your deals? When you can fall for chains of silver You can fall for chains of gold You can fall for pretty strangers And the promises they hold You promised me everything You promised me thick and thin, yeah Now you just say 'Oh Romeo, yeah You know I used to have a scene with him'.
Chorus 2:	Juliet, when we made love you used to cry You said 'I love you like the stars above I'll love you till I die' There's a place for us, you know the movie song When you gonna realise, It was just that the time was wrong Juliet.

Verse 3:	I can't do the talks Like they talk on the T.V. And I can't do a love song Like the way it's meant to be I can't do everything But I'll do anything for you I can't do anything 'cept be in love with you. And all I do is miss you And the way we used to be All I do is keep the beat And bad company And all I do is kiss you Through the bars of a rhyme Julie, I'd do the stars with you Anytime.
Chorus 3:	As Chorus 2

131

Wild Wood

Words & Music by Paul Weller

Capo 2nd fret (optional)

1 bar count in:

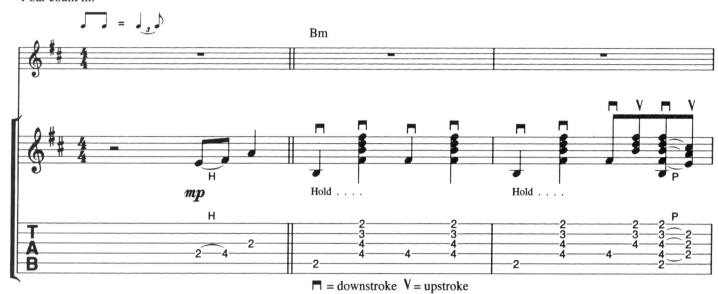

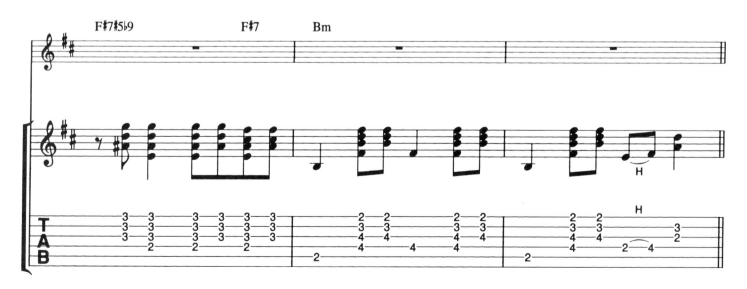

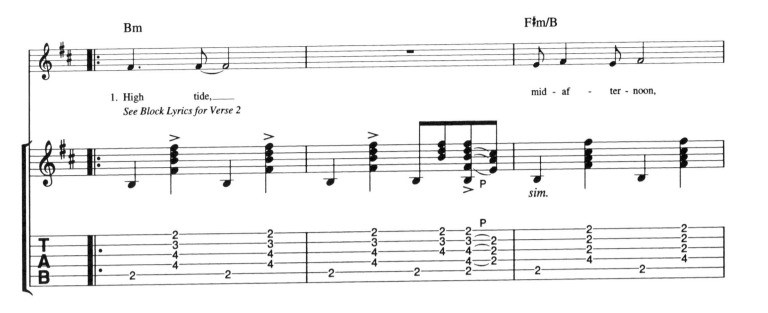

1. High tide,____ mid - af - ter - noon,

See Block Lyrics for Verse 2

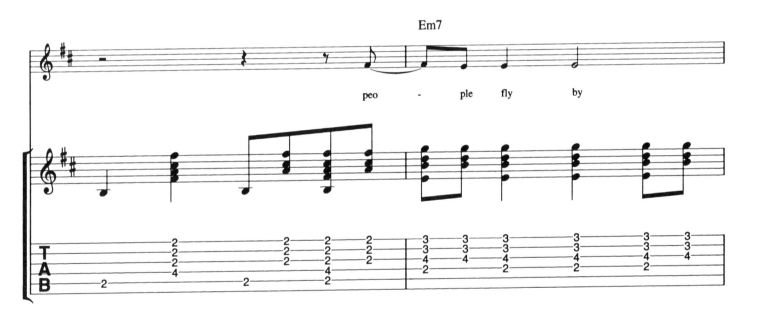

peo - ple fly by

in the traf - fic's boom.____

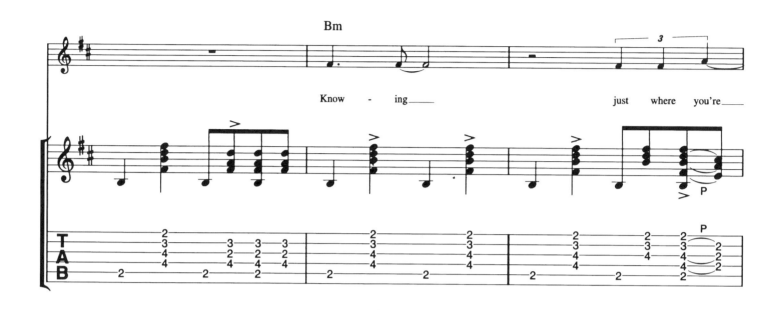

Know - ing___ just where you're___

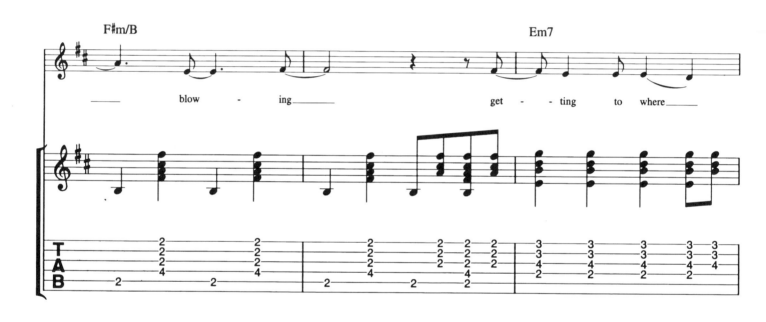

blow - ing___ get - - ting to where___

you___ should be go - ing.___

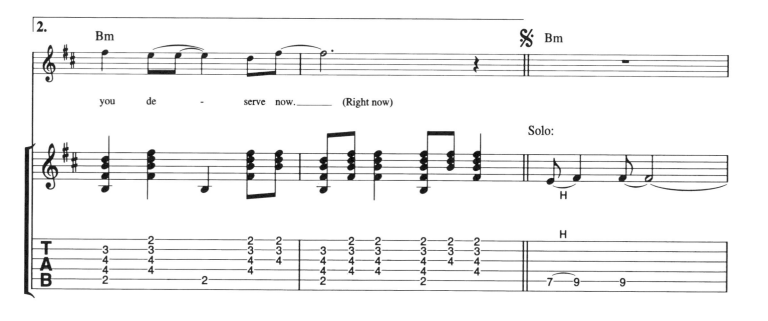

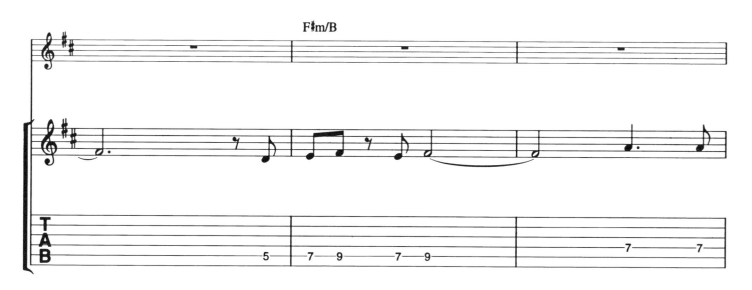

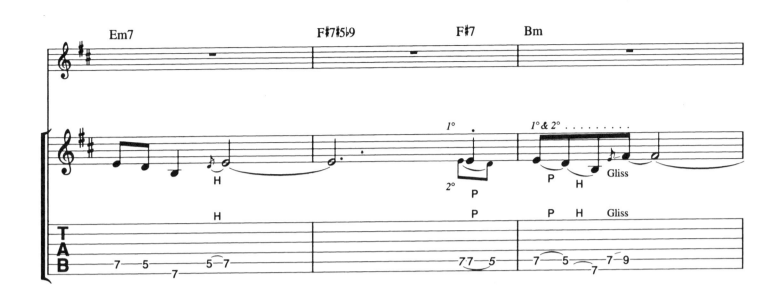

Verse:

3. Climb - ing_____ for - ev - er_____

_____ try - ing_____ find your way out

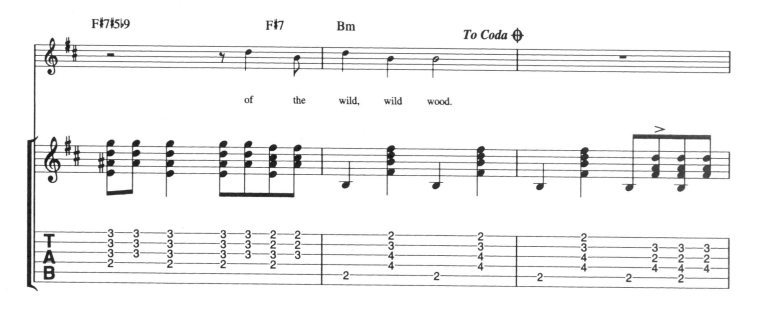

of the wild, wild wood.

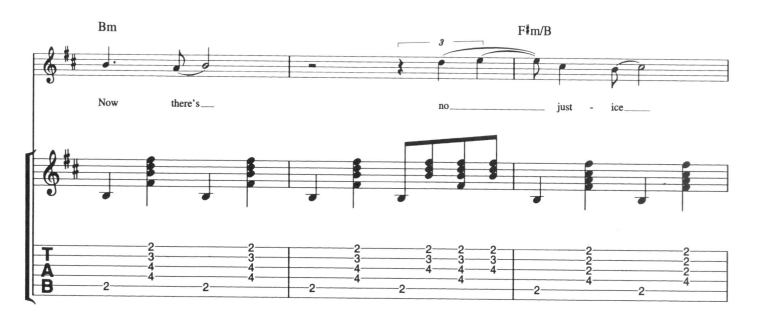

Now there's   no   just - ice

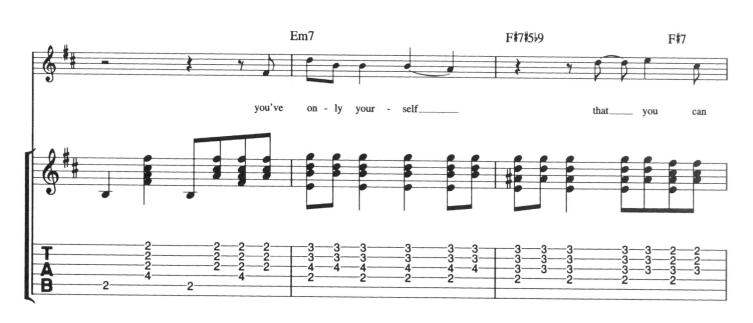

you've on - ly your - self   that   you can

trust___ in.___ And I say___

Said you're gon-na find your way out of the

wild,___ wild___ wood.___

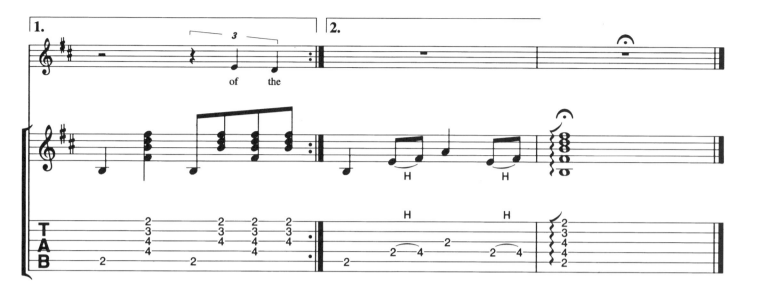

of   the

Verse 2:
Don't let them get you down
Making you feel guilty about
Golden rain will bring you riches
All the good things you deserve now.

Verse 4:
And I said high tide, mid-afternoon
People fly by in the traffic's boom
Knowing just where you're blowing
Getting to where you should be going.

Verse 5(%):
Day by day your world fades away
Waking to feel all the dreams that say
Golden rain will bring you riches
All the good things you deserve now.

Verse 6
And I say climbing, forever trying
You're gonna find your way out of the wold, wild wood.
(To Coda)

Wonderwall

Words & Music by Noel Gallagher

* Symbols in parentheses represent chord names with respect to capoed gtr (Tab 0 = 2nd fret)
  Symbols above represent actual sounding chords.

1. To-day is gon-na be the day that they're gon-na throw it back to you,
2. Back beat, the word is on the street that the fire in your heart is out.
3. To-day was gon-na be the day but they'll nev-er throw it back to you,

by now, you should have some-how re-a-lised what you got-ta do.
I'm sure you've heard it all be-fore but you never real-ly had a doubt.
by now, you should have some-how re-a-lised what you've not to do.

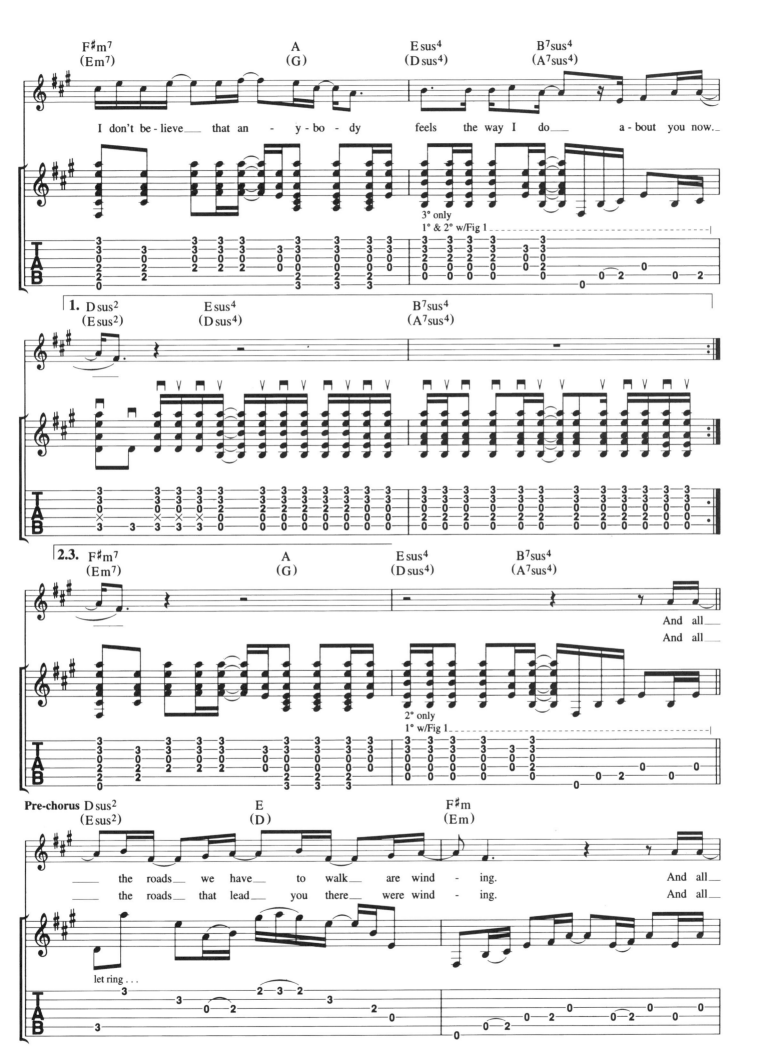

I don't be-lieve___ that an — y-bo — dy feels the way I do___ a-bout you now.

3° only
1° & 2° w/Fig 1

1. D sus² (E sus²)   E sus⁴ (D sus⁴)   B⁷sus⁴ (A⁷sus⁴)

2.3. F♯m⁷ (Em⁷)   A (G)   E sus⁴ (D sus⁴)   B⁷sus⁴ (A⁷sus⁴)

And all___
And all___

2° only
1° w/Fig 1

Pre-chorus D sus² (E sus²)   E (D)   F♯m (Em)

___ the roads___ we have___ to walk___ are wind — ing.
___ the roads___ that lead___ you there___ were wind — ing.

And all___
And all___

let ring . . .

142

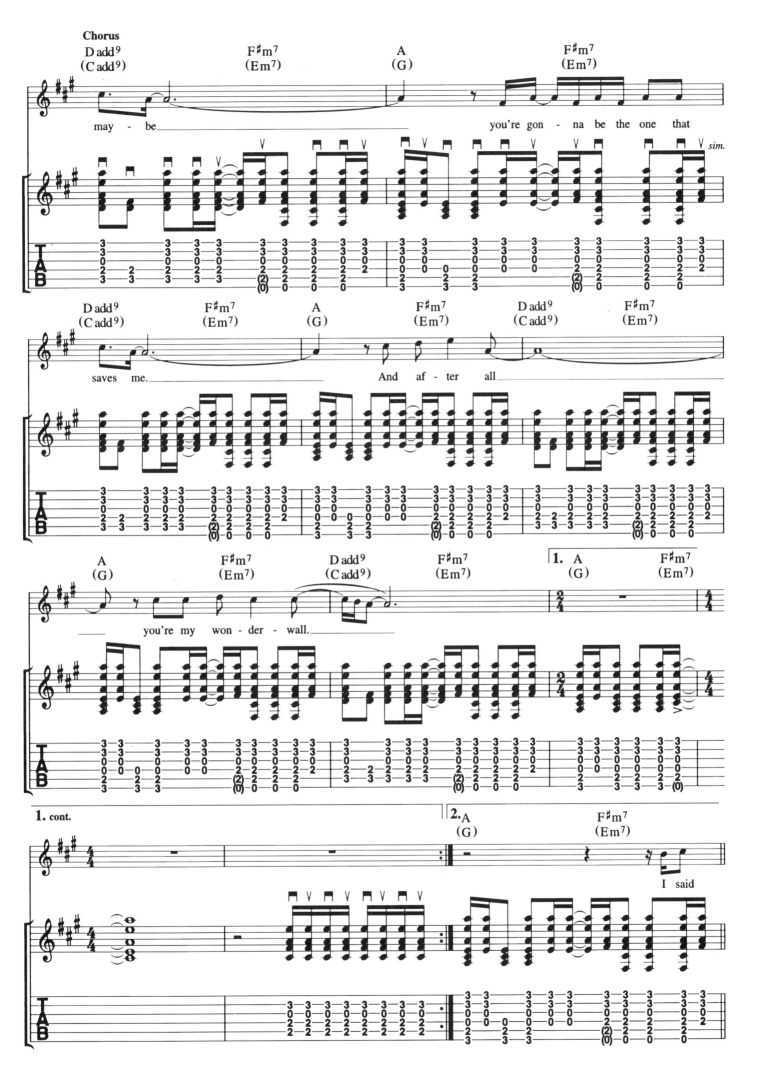

Outro chorus

may - be___

(I said___ may - be.)___

you're gon - na be the one that

saves___ me.___

And af - ter all___

you're my won - der - wall.___

I said

144

Wanted Dead Or Alive

Words & Music by Jon Bon Jovi & Richie Sambora

Intro

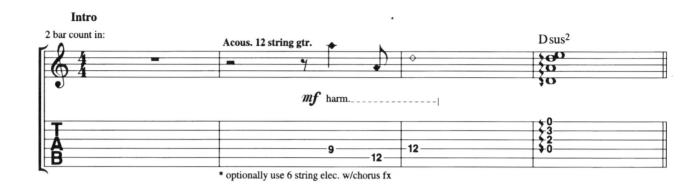

* optionally use 6 string elec. w/chorus fx

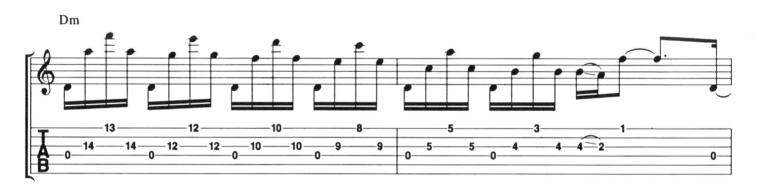

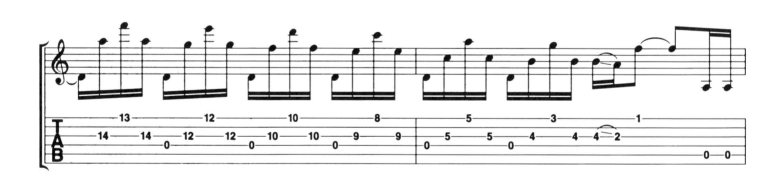

Printed in Malta by Progress Press Co. Ltd.   9/10 (175659)